JACK BE NIMBLE, JACK BE DEAD

A Penny Preston Mystery

WENDY ALLEN

Four Bean Soup LLC

To my mother, Linda Louise Allen
"Motherhood: All love begins and ends there." — **Robert Browning**

I am loved, I am a mother, I am a wife, I am a creator, I am strong, I am a child of God, and I am all of these things because of the seeds you planted and nurtured with your warmth. Thank you will never be enough.

॰

NEWSLETTER

Do you want to make sure you don't miss any upcoming releases or giveaways? Be sure to sign up for my newsletter at http://wendyowensbooks.com/

~

CHAPTER ONE

I'VE SEEN a lot of things during my thirty-three years. Until today, a dead body had not been one of them. I suspect the image of Jack Egerton face as he lay on the floor dead from a knife in his back, will be permanently etched in my brain. A picture I will go to sleep thinking about and wake up remembering for the rest of my life.

The oven timer began to buzz. I sighed, remembering what I'd been doing before my day took a horrible detour.

Sheriff Wright cleared his throat, and I could feel his eyes fixed on me as I crossed the room to the oven. I slipped floral print oven mitts onto my hands and removed the three pans of freshly baked banana bread, placing them on the counter behind me to cool. He rocked onto his toes to see what I was doing; a scowl planted firmly on his weathered face.

"Something wrong Sheriff?" I asked.

He shrugged. "Just curious, did you decide to bake a bunch of bread before or after you found the dead body in the back of your shop?"

I shifted my brown eyes in his direction. "Willard," I used his first name to remind him who he was talking to. I grew up visiting my aunts in this town my entire childhood, and after my divorce, I moved here to live with one of them. I took over her business, the Half Day Coffeehouse when she died three years ago, and Sheriff Willard Wright has been one of my best customers ever since. "Don't you recognize the smell?"

The corners of his mouth softened, and his tongue escaped, moistening his lips. He glanced over his shoulder, ensuring we were alone, then shifted his weight from one foot to the other. "Is that your famous banana bread?"

"It sure is, would you like a slice?" I offered.

"I'm on the job, Penny," Sheriff Wright halfheartedly protested. "That wouldn't look very professional of me."

I lowered my voice and gave the sheriff a sympathetic look. "He's not getting any deader. Come on. I'll cut a piece for you while it's still warm. How's June?"

June was the Sheriff's wife, and despite being the exact picture perfect image of what you would imagine a pleasant round grandmother who spent her days baking in the kitchen to look like, she could not cook. Down to her lace apron, June tried to play the part, but no matter how many attempts she made she always managed to burn even the simplest of recipes. I remember one time I gave her the recipe for my easy-peasy peanut butter cookies: one egg, one cup of sugar, and one cup peanut butter, roll into balls, flatten and bake at 350 degrees for ten minutes. It doesn't get much simpler than that. When I asked Sheriff Wright the next day how it went, he described how the cookies had all melted into one another to form a massive sheet of what he described as burnt brittle.

"I suppose a slice wouldn't hurt—I did skip breakfast," he acquiesced before adding in a firmer tone, "You really should be taking this seriously, Penny."

"I found a man murdered this morning; I can assure you, Willard, I am taking this very seriously," I answered him before carefully removing a warm slice of banana bread and placing it on a plain white plate, and handing it to him.

Sheriff Wright eyed me suspiciously. "Tell me what happened and leave nothing out."

"We've already gone over this," I moaned, not wishing to relive the morning again.

"We're going to go over it again," the Sheriff said sternly before shoving a bite of the steaming hot banana bread into his mouth. He winced from the heat, then made an "o" shape with his mouth, attempting to cool the food in his mouth by sucking air in.

I smirked. "Careful. It's hot."

The bell hanging on the front door chimed, and I scrunched my face, annoyed that I didn't remember to lock it after the Sheriff arrived. I leaned to one side, preparing to tell the would-be customer that we were closed due to ... well, I suppose I could say the dead body in the back of the store, but that certainly wouldn't be good for business. Emergency. Yes, emergency would be a good word to use. I opened my mouth but the words stuck in my throat when I saw it wasn't a customer. It was Deputy Handsome—I mean Hanson.

Sheriff Wright choked on a cluster of crumbs from the banana bread he was devouring and shoved the plate onto the back of the counter. "Derrick, will you lock that blasted door? The entire building is a crime scene."

"Yes, sir, Sheriff Wright," he replied, turning and flipping the deadbolt.

"Should I put a sign up that says we'll be closed today?" I offered.

"Derrick can do that," the Sheriff replied.

Deputy Hanson approached the counter hurriedly, a concerned look on his face. "You okay Ms. Preston?" No matter how many times I told Deputy Hanson to call me Penny, he always insisted that if he were in uniform, he would call me by my last name. I suppose that's why I rarely called him Derrick.

Deputy Hanson was the opposite of my ex-husband. He was polite, caring, loyal, and wow, was he easy on the eyes. Okay, my ex was a looker too, but none of those other things. If I wasn't so bad at relationships, I could see Deputy Hanson earning the title of most eligible bachelor for me, but I am cursed in the personal relationships department.

"I'm fine," I lied as I pulled out a pen, paper, and tape from under the counter and handed it to him. Derrick Hanson was hot. There was no mistaking that. I'm 5'9", and his muscular frame towers well above mine. He keeps his dark hair short, and his beard trimmed neatly. If his smoldering eyes weren't enough to finish off the package he is also one of the sweetest and most tenderhearted men I have ever met. That being said, I am still searching for what is wrong with him. After all, thirty-five years old and unmarried—there must be something defective with Deputy Hanson.

"Okay, let's go over this again," Sheriff Wright huffed impatiently as he took a seat on one of the bar stools across from me, his notepad and pencil out. "Tell me exactly—Why didn't you notice the body when you came in?"

"Because, if I entered through the back it wakes the dogs up and I don't have time to walk them all as soon as I get in," I grumbled. "If I want the pastries done in time for opening, I come straight in the front and get everything into the oven, just like I did with the banana bread today. Then I take the dogs for a quick walk and feed them."

Aunt Lily owned the building, and when she died, she willed the entire kit and caboodle to me. There's the seamstress, Linda Louise, upstairs. The back part of the first floor was a dog grooming business, Pups and Suds. When the grooming business owner decided to close shop and retire to Arizona to be closer to their grandchildren, rather than rent the space again I decided to use it as a small animal rescue. The space wasn't huge, and I couldn't take in more than ten to twelve dogs at a time, but it at least gave a few more dogs a chance to find a home. My coffee shop—Half Day Coffee-house—occupied the storefront and took up most of the bottom floor of the building. The coffee shop was also the perfect opportunity to talk to the prospective future owners about the pets in the shelter.

"So you came in through the front?" the Sheriff clarified.

I nodded, "That's what I said, just like every other morning."

"You got the banana bread into the oven and then what did you do?" the Sheriff questioned.

I glanced over at Derrick who was finishing up the sign for the window. The sign read: Sorry, closed today for an emergency. He grabbed the tape and made his way to the entrance where customers were already beginning to gather and chatter outside the locked door.

"What do you think they're saying?" I groaned.

Willard looked out at the small group of onlookers as Derrick finished taping up the sign. Derrick then made his way to each window and closed the blinds, leaving the window in the front door as the only place to sneak a peek, for those who were bold enough.

"Penny, you were seen arguing with the deceased. I would worry more about the corpse in the back of your shop than what a bunch of looky loos are saying," Willard warned sternly.

I gasped, shocked by what I was hearing. "Arguing, what are you talking about? Who saw us arguing?"

Willard furrowed his brow, his frustration was evident. "Oh come on Penny, half the town saw it. Heck, Derrick and I were in here having our morning coffee when you laid into Jack Egerton."

I pursed my lips and stood perfectly still for a moment, the uncomfortable silence swallowing me. "I wasn't arguing. I was just telling him that he wasn't going to get away with what he did."

"Some might say that sounds like a threat," Sheriff Wright added pointedly.

"You think I killed him?" The words felt like lead as they left my lips and my shoulders sank in defeat at the idea I could even be a suspect.

"Nobody said that," Deputy Hanson interjected as he reached out to touch my arm and then quickly thought better of the action and pulled back. "We just need to know everything."

"I've told you everything!" I exclaimed. "I mean I guess maybe it got a little heated yesterday, but I would never—" my words trailed off as I recounted the interaction with Jack, the town dog catcher.

"What exactly was the argument about?" Willard inquired, in a softer tone. I assumed he could see how rattled I was becoming by the direction of the questioning.

I frowned because the conversation I'd had with Jack still made my blood boil. "Mrs. Dumont called me to see if the dog she had asked Jack to pick up and deliver was doing all right. The problem was, Jack never delivered a dog to me. When he came in yesterday for some coffee, I asked him where the Bernese Mountain Dog was that Mrs. Dumont asked him to bring me. At first, he acted like he didn't know what I was talking about. When I pressed him, he said he took it to the city shelter like he was supposed to."

"Well maybe he did," Sheriff Wright suggested.

I shook my head. "Nope, I'd already called the city shelter. I told Jack that and that's when he got really mad. He told me I had no right to question him doing his job. I reminded him that Mrs. Dumont has the right—as a

Wyoming citizen—to request a stray she finds inside the city limits be delivered to my shelter instead of the cities since mine is a no-kill shelter. I informed him he was violating a city ordinance."

"You reminded him, huh?" The Sheriff scoffed.

"Okay, maybe I reminded him in a very firm tone," I shrugged.

"But why would Jack lie?" the Sheriff inquired, his voice heavy with skepticism.

"You tell me," I snapped, frustrated. "Sorry Sheriff. It's been one heck of a morning."

"Don't worry Penny, we're going to figure out who did this," Deputy Hanson attempted to reassure me.

In the kennel area, we heard a shriek that caused us to jump, and I saw the Deputy reach for his gun out of the corner of my eye. I winced as I realized I had forgotten to warn Linda about the body in the kennel.

"That must be Mrs. Louise," I said, my eyes darting to the Sheriff. The Deputy released his hand from his gun. "She volunteers to help me walk and feed the dogs each morning."

Looking at Deputy Hanson, Sheriff Wright nodded toward the door that led to the kennel. "Will you check on her Derrick?"

"Yes, sir," Deputy Hanson replied, heading in the direction they all heard the cry.

Sheriff Wright immediately looked back at me and asked, "She has a key?"

My eyes widened as I repeatedly blinked, a surprised look peeling across my face. "Yes, but I doubt a sixty-year-old seamstress was the one who planted a knife in Jack's back."

"Who else has a key?" he pressed, his expression hardening again.

It took me a minute to process the question. It suddenly dawned on me I was reviewing possible suspects in a murder case with Sheriff Wright. It felt like this conversation had to be a dream.

"I don't know. My cousin Brayden I suppose." Brayden, Aunt Bridgett's son, was my tech guy. He ran the computer repair business in town, the only computer repair in town in fact.

My family had history in this town. My mom, Anne, and both of her sisters were born and raised here. Wyoming, Ohio is the town that everyone comes back to eventually, my mom would say. But not her, she was determined not to be another townie. She lives in California where she runs an art gallery. She still can't understand why I wanted to move back here, but the things she hated about this small town are the things I love. Aunt Lily, God rest her soul, she got me. She understood that I needed this town, even if I couldn't understand why. My Aunt Bridgett, Brayden's mom, had lived here her entire life, until her husband, Uncle Joe passed away. That's when she moved to Florida, insisting that another Midwest winter would have her joining Uncle Joe.

Sheriff Wright scribbled down Brayden's name alongside where he had already written Linda. I rubbed my forehead, uncomfortable I had just named my cousin as a suspect in a murder. "Brayden didn't do this; he barely knew Jack. Plus, you know all these people, Sheriff Wright. They're not killers."

"I'm not saying Brayden murdered Jack," Sheriff Wright's face was void of expression. "I need to talk to everyone that could have possibly seen something. You never know, if they had a key and were here for another reason they could have clues to who did this and not even know."

"Penny!" I heard Linda gasp as she emerged from behind the door that led to the kennel. "Thank God you're okay." She made her way around the counter and scooped me up into the tightest hug I have ever received. Linda stood a good six inches shorter than me, and her short gray hair tickled my chin.

"I'm fine," I assured her, as I pulled away, trying to catch my breath. "I wasn't here when it happened."

"Deputy, can you wait with the body for the Coroner to arrive? The last thing we need is someone else stumbling in and contaminating the crime scene," Sheriff Wright grumbled, making his frustration very clear. Even though we were a small town, we had our very own Coroner, Dwight Beetlesbee. At least we had one when said Coroner wasn't fishing, golfing, or hunting. Quite the sportsman, Dwight Beetlesbee.

Linda glared at the Sheriff. "And where exactly were you, Sheriff Wright, when this man was murdered in Penny's shop?"

"Excuse me?" he gasped in disbelief.

"Our Penny could have been another victim of this cowardly murderer. Why weren't you out doing your job and patrolling the streets?"

"Now you listen here—" Sheriff Wright started backtracking in his deep voice, obviously flustered.

"Linda, there was no way Sheriff Wright could have known someone had broken into the kennel. He's here now, doing his job, and we need to help him." I looked at the Sheriff to see if his furrowed brows had softened at all. If they had, it wasn't noticeable.

He huffed before he glared disapprovingly one last time at Linda. She huffed right back at him. "Does anyone else have a key?"

I cocked my head to the side, looking up at the ceiling as I tried to recall everyone who had a key to the kennel. "Aunt Bridgett, but she's in Florida, Ms. Shaw from the library, she takes some volunteer shifts with the dogs, and ... yeah, I think that's it."

Derrick popped his head through the partially open front door. "Dwight's here."

"Okay, help him with anything he needs," Sheriff Wright replied before standing.

"Would you like a cup of coffee to wash that banana bread down Sheriff?" I offered.

He nodded. "In a 'to go' cup?"

"Of course," I replied with a smile, pouring the cup and adding one cream and two sugars—how I knew he liked his coffee—and then handed it to him.

"Penny, we're not done. I may have more questions for you, so don't leave town," he instructed.

Linda snickered and then said, "Where's she gonna go Sheriff? Make a run for the border?"

"You know what I mean," he grunted.

"Yes, Sheriff. I know exactly what you mean. I just want you to catch whoever did this," I intervened, staring hard at Linda before turning to the Sheriff with a sincere and hopeful look on my face.

Sheriff Wright picked up his coffee, walked to the door that led to the kennel and closed it behind him. I didn't follow. I would be happy never to see another dead body as long as I lived.

≈

CHAPTER TWO

"LOOK AT THEM OUT THERE, like a bunch of vultures," Linda huffed as she peeked through the slats of the blinds of the coffee shop before returning to my side.

"Oh come on, it's not like there's ever much excitement in this town, can you blame them?" Wyoming was where you moved to raise a family. With one of the best schools in the state and a tightly knit, safe community—until last night that is—it was easy to see its appeal and the many things the city had to offer.

"What are we going to do?" she asked, squeezing my arm. She seemed agitated.

"What do you mean?" I inquired, confused by her question. "I'm going to plastic wrap this banana bread to keep it fresh, so I can sell it tomorrow. You know, when I don't have a dead body in the back of my store."

"No," she huffed, shaking her head. "How are we going to find the killer?"

My stomach lurched as I failed to hide the shock on my face. "How are we going to what?" I choked out, eyes wide as I stared at her.

"Oh, come on. It was evident you're Sheriff Wright's number one suspect."

"It was?" I gasped, wishing I was a drinker right then. Perhaps a stiff drink was exactly what I needed to calm my nerves.

"Of course, you have to find the killer yourself, or you'll end up finding yourself railroaded for a crime you didn't commit," Linda chattered on.

"I will not," I exclaimed, pretending I wasn't worried that she was right. "I've known Sheriff Willard and June since I was a kid. There's no way he would ever think I was capable of such a terrible thing. They'll figure out who did this."

"And if they don't?" Linda questioned, drumming her fingernails on the counter. "This is a small town, people talk, they'll want someone to be punished for this."

"You've been reading too many crime novels," I suggested, making my way around her and pouring myself a big glass of water. I gulped it down, trying to calm myself. This was, in fact, a true statement as Linda was the head of the local Mystery Readers Book Club.

"Okay, fine. Don't believe me, but did you ever think that maybe all those mystery novels I read makes me a bit of an expert?" There was no laughter in her voice. Linda considered herself an expert. She sighed, her head dropping to one side.

"Let's leave this one to the professionals, okay?"

"But if you had to guess," she pressed, her eyes fixed on me, and her arms now crossed over her chest.

I considered the question, though I couldn't let Linda know that. The truth was, I had no idea who could have possibly killed Jack. "If I had to guess what?"

"Who killed him," Linda continued in a strained whisper.

"You just saw a dead body, how are you not more disturbed?" I huffed, running my fingers through my hair and trying my hardest to avoid her question.

She shrugged. "Of course it was disturbing, but pretty much what I expected a dead body would look like. Well," she hesitated as she paused in thought for a moment. "I suppose I thought there would be more blood."

I gave a slight chuff. "Something is not right about you Linda."

"Did Piper see what happened?" Piper is my personal pet, a Dachshund with an eating disorder. She would eat herself to death if I allowed it. I measure each of her meals carefully to ensure she doesn't binge herself into a food coma.

"She goes home with me at night, how could she have seen anything?" I asked, crossing over to retrieve a damp towel from under the counter and wipe the same countertop I had already cleaned three times that morning. I wasn't a neat freak, but when I was stressed cleaning gave me a purpose to focus on, at least temporarily.

"Maybe you could get her to communicate with some of the other dogs and see if they saw anything," Linda suggested. Linda is one of the few people who knows about my strange connection with Pipe. When Piper and I were moving here from California, we slid off the road during one of the lovely Midwest winter storms and were trapped together in a snowbank. We nearly died, stuck there for days before someone found us. Since then, I've had a link with Piper. I know, it sounds crazy, but it's true. I've even shown Linda by her holding up a message to Piper in one room, and I can read it in another room. Piper can send me images of what she's thinking. Admittedly, it's usually flashes of bacon or the occasional plate of sausage and biscuits.

I glanced over at Piper who was sleeping in her bed under the counter. The excitement of the morning apparently had not bothered her. "Yeah, and if she can figure something out how exactly do I tell Sheriff Wright about that? Uh, hey, Sheriff. I have a psychic connection with my dog, and she has some information she wants me to relay to you that could break the case wide open," I said with heavy sarcasm.

"It wouldn't hurt," Linda encouraged, her eyes locking onto mine. "I mean what if the killer is someone you know? What if it's someone you serve every day? What if the killer is really after you?"

"Why would anyone want to kill me?" I gasped, taking a step back and tossing the damp towel into the towel bucket.

"Wouldn't you want to know?" she chimed, eyebrows raised.

I relented because she had a point. If there were a reason for me to be looking over my shoulder constantly, I would like to know. I threw up my hands before slapping the outside of my legs in a defeated gesture. "Fine, when the Sheriff and everyone else leaves, we'll see if Piper can get anything out of the other dogs."

I knew for a fact that Piper had conversations with other dogs. This was what started me opening the kennel in the first place. After coming across a stray on a chilly fall morning, Piper relayed some of the thoughts from the stray. He had been scared, and alone, and hungry. I remembered the aching feeling deep inside as Piper projected the thoughts from the sad animal into my mind. That day I took the For Rent sign down in the grooming shop window and began with my plan to open the kennel as a temporary home for the strays I came across.

Linda gave a triumphant pump of her fist at her side. "Yes," she hissed. "You're doing the right thing."

"All I've agreed to do so far is asked Piper to find out if the other dogs saw something. Don't get ahead of yourself," I warned her, not wanting her to get her hopes up.

"How many times was he stabbed?" Linda asked after a moment of silence, her wide eyes and the way she leaned in closer made her look like a kid on Christmas morning, waiting to see what was in the beautifully wrapped presents under the tree.

The sound of my phone ringing and vibrating on the countertop made me jump. I saw Brayden's name flashing on the screen. News traveled fast in a small town, I can only assume he was calling to check on me. I clicked the button on the side of my phone to send it to voicemail. I didn't have it in me to explain the situation to another living soul.

I sighed, distracted. "What did you say again?"

"I asked if you knew how many times he had been stabbed," she repeated, her face red with frustration.

"What? I don't know, how would I know that?" I choked on my words.

"You were alone with the body all that time, and you didn't look?" she asked me, sincerely surprised by my lack of curiosity.

"First of all, I called the Sheriff as soon as I found Jack, so I wasn't alone very long with him. Second, I don't have any desire to know all the gruesome details of a homicide like you do. Much less when it's someone I know." Linda could drive me absolutely crazy, but I loved that old bat more than anything. When my Aunt passed away, she was the one who helped me decide to keep the coffee shop running. She also was the one that encouraged the dog shelter when everyone else in town thought it was a crazy idea.

"I wouldn't say I need to know but aren't you even the slightest bit curious, who killed him?" Linda was practically grinding her teeth in anticipation.

"I suppose, thanks to you."

"What did I do?" she squealed, pulling her shoulders back as if shocked by my statement.

"You've freaked me out that some psycho killer is stalking me," I huffed.

She shook her head, correcting me. "I never said a killer

was stalking you. I merely wondered out loud if you would like to know if there was one."

"Geez, Linda. Thanks, that's much better," I added, making sure she could see my eyes roll from her vantage point.

"I wonder what time he was killed," she said, ignoring my previous reaction.

"It had to be after eleven," I replied glancing up at the clock and then back at Linda. "That was when I stopped in to give the dogs their last walk of the night, and there was no dead body on the ground."

Linda scrunched her shoulders up by her ears and was whispering again, "I wonder if he was lurking in the shadows, watching you, waiting to—"

"Will you stop it!" I demanded, slapping the counter with an open palm. "You're—you're going to scare Piper," I lied. We both glanced over to see Piper give us a quick eye roll in response to hearing her name before she settled back into her nap with a huff.

"All right. If you had to guess, who would you think did it?" Linda continued, relentless in her pursuit of a mystery.

"You're not going to stop, are you?" I muttered.

"Nope," she shook her head wildly. "So you might as well play along."

"Hmmm..." I started, trying to consider her question seriously. Honestly, I didn't know Jack Egerton very well. I had seen him out and about with a girlfriend a while back, and then I stopped seeing her with him and started seeing him with a new girl who was much plainer. The newer girlfriend seemed much sweeter, always offering a smile when we would pass on the street and she was eager to pet any dog I was walking. "Seriously, I have no idea. Who do you think did it?"

"Well, I mean, if this were a murder mystery the most obvious suspect would be you," she started, shrugging as if she couldn't help that these were the facts. "After all, he was found in your shop, and you had recently had an argument with the deceased."

"I did not argue with him and will you please not call him the deceased," I half-shouted at Linda.

"Isn't that what he is?"

"Yes, but that doesn't make it any less morbid," I lowered my voice to a whisper.

Linda laughed, waving a hand in my direction dismissively, "I think that ship has sailed. He's dead, that's just a fact."

I growled in frustration, "And doesn't anyone in this town have anything else to talk about other than a discussion I had with the dog catcher?"

Linda smirked. "No, we don't. We honestly don't. Since we're going to assume the killer isn't you—"

"Because it isn't," I interjected, eyebrows raised.

Linda tilted her head and pursed her lips before stating, "If it was, I doubt you would admit it, would you? So, hypothetically, let's assume it wasn't you. Who else would have a motive?"

"An angry pet owner?" I suggested, knowing that it was a crazy idea before the words left my mouth. I continued with the thought nonetheless. "Maybe Jack took someone's dog to a kill shelter and then they were...oh, I can't even say it."

Linda shook her head and sighed, "Yeah, you're not the killer. You can't even talk about animals being put to—"

"Stop!" I interrupted her, raising a hand in protest. "You don't need to say it."

"We all know you love dogs, but somehow I doubt a pet owner would kill someone over a dog. And why kill Jack here? What was he even doing in the kennel? Is there anyone you can think of who has it out for you?"

I sighed and narrowed my brow as I contemplated the question. "I don't think so. Maybe it was a crime of opportunity." I met Linda's gaze; I could see the wheels were spinning, and her detective hat was securely in place.

"Was anything taken?"

"Nooo," I let the one word drag out. "The Sheriff asked me the same question."

"So, it wasn't a robbery gone wrong," she said. She pinched her lip between her thumb and forefinger as she thought about other alternatives.

"Then who could have killed him?" I asked as I shifted my feet, pressing my body against the counter. There was a dense fog in my brain. Then cutting through like a bolt of lightning came the realization that we were having a conversation about who murdered a man in my dog kennel. It felt like it had to be a terrible nightmare.

"Mac Murdock," Linda announced in a bold and confident voice as if she had just unmasked the killer in an episode of Scooby Doo.

"Old Mr. Murdock? Isn't he like a hundred years old?" I asked, a doubtful scowl plastered on my face.

"Seventy-four and that's not that old," she rebutted as she crossed her arms.

"I guess not ... if you're sixty," I grinned, waiting for her reaction.

"Hey, he's spry for an old guy," she added, not taking the bait.

Linda was easily a foot shorter than me, but she wasn't the type of woman you messed with. She reminded me of a pit bull, ready to devour anyone who messed with the people she cared about. I relented and asked the question I knew she was eagerly waiting for me to ask. "Okay fine. What reason would Mac Murdock have to kill Jack Egerton?"

She slapped her hands together before revealing, "Jealousy of course. Jack beat Mac in the last election for dog catcher."

"Didn't Mac retire?" I asked skeptically, wrapping the last

loaf of banana bread and securing it on the shelf at the far end of the counter.

"Oh no," Linda clarified shaking her head. "He ran, and Jack beat him in a landslide."

"Okay. First, I doubt it was a landslide because I didn't even know that was an elected position until now, so I doubt many people cared enough to vote on the matter. Second, Mac has been in for coffee, and he hasn't seemed very broken up about not being dog catcher anymore," I argued.

"Perhaps he's just good at hiding his feelings," Linda muttered. "I say we talk to him."

"What?" I gasped, shocked by her suggestion. "No, we were just talking in hypotheticals. You never said anything about talking to people."

"It's not like we're going to question him, just have a neighborly chat. Come on, please? What harm could it do?" Linda pleaded.

I leaned against the counter with my hip. "I don't know. Is that even legal?"

"Talking to your neighbors, what would possibly be illegal about that? Trust me; nothing could go wrong," Linda smiled confidently. I was certain she was mistaken.

∾

CHAPTER THREE

THE CORONER, Sheriff, Deputy, and the cleanup crew took several hours to finish their work in the kennel. By the time Linda and I were allowed to walk the dogs, they were all whining.

"Thanks for staying and helping me," I said to Linda as we divided the dogs into two groups and leashed them up.

"Are you kidding me, and miss all the excitement?" Linda exclaimed.

We exited the back of the building, down the rear steps. A small crowd was still gathered at the front of the coffee shop, hoping to pick up a little piece of gossip to spread.

"We better go down the alley and cut through the school parking lot to get to the park," I suggested.

"Good idea," Linda agreed. "I think this may be the most excitement this little town has seen since Parker Mayweather ate himself to death at the all you can eat Sunday buffet."

I laughed. "You're terrible. He did not."

"He did so!" Linda argued. "That man ate himself straight into a heart attack, what would you call it?"

"You make it sound like he ate until he exploded."

"Not much difference if you ask me," she shrugged, her arm jerking from the six dogs on leashes practically walking her.

I kept a shorter lead on the six leashes in my hand, but with Piper next to me I rarely had to worry about any pulling. She was always keeping an eye out, making sure everyone walked in an orderly fashion, nudging any wandering pups back in line with her long snout. Piper strolled along, her short legs walking hurriedly next to me to keep up with my stride.

"What do you think happened to that Mountain Dog Mrs. Dumont told Jack about yesterday?" I asked, unable to shake why Jack would lie to me about capturing a stray.

"Who knows," Linda grumbled, moving the dogs onto the sidewalk. "Do you think that had anything to do with why he was killed?"

"I can't imagine what," I replied.

"Is it an expensive breed? Maybe he found out who the owner was and tried to squeeze them for money," Linda suggested, salivating over the juicy details of her make-believe story.

"They're not a rare breed, but I know a lot of dog owners live for their pets. I suppose if one of them felt like their pet were threatened enough it could come to blows."

"Gee, no kidding?" Linda taunted me.

"If you're insinuating the relationship between Piper and me is that way, you know very well she isn't just a pet," I reminded her. "She's family. When we get to the park, I'll see what she can find out from the other dogs."

"I don't know why you don't tell more people about the connection you and Piper have," Linda's lips twitched.

"Because most people would think I was crazy," I replied letting out a bark of a laugh.

"I think you're insane and I still love you," Linda chimed,

bursting out in front of me, the dogs making a run for the park that was in sight and taking her with them.

I forced a grin, and called after her, "Gee, thanks, Linda."

"You know what I mean." She glanced over her shoulder, ensuring I could hear. "People wouldn't understand them until you show them that it's real like you showed me."

The Channel Nine news truck drove past as we reached the park, heading in the direction of my coffee shop.

"Think that's for you?" Linda asked.

"Are you kidding? Why else would they come to Wyoming?" And I was right. I loved Wyoming for that exact reason. We had a total of two stop lights, and the sidewalks were practically rolled up by nine p.m. Everything that drove me nuts about living in a small town were also the things I loved about living here.

As soon as we stepped foot onto the grass, the dogs began to play. As the other's ran off to frolic with one another, I lowered myself to my knees to get as close as I could to eye level with Piper. "Hey, girl. I bet today has been pretty confusing for you, huh?"

She pressed her head against my hand as I pet her before jumping up on her hind legs to quickly swipe her tongue against my nose. "I love you, too," I added. "I need you to do me a big favor, girl. A man was hurt last night in front of the other dogs—"

Linda snickered as she cleared her throat and said, "Yeah, hurt with a big knife." My head jerked in her direction as I glared up at her. She raised her hands in surrender. "Okay, sorry, I'll shut up."

"Can you talk to the other dogs and let me know if they saw anything?" I asked. Piper immediately turned, and with her tail wagging, she ran to join the others.

I stood watching silently.

"Well?" Linda barked.

"Well, what?"

"Did it work?" Linda asked.

"I guess we'll find out soon enough," I answered, my eyes drifting toward the dogs. We both stood and watched as the dogs shared sniffs, pawing at one another, and offered a mixture of whines and growls.

"Is that what it sounds like when they talk?" Linda inquired, implying because I had a psychic connection with my dog, I was suddenly the world's leading expert on all dogs everywhere.

I lifted my shoulders to my ears, before dropping them back down in place. "How am I supposed to know?"

"Well, you're the dog whisperer," she grunted.

"It's not like we have a conversation in dog speak," I laughed. "It's more like she can put images in my mind."

"That's so cool," she grinned, as she continued to watch the animals interact. One began to sniff Piper's backside. "I wonder what that means."

"I'm not sure I want to know," I crinkled my nose at the display.

Just then an image of Jack flashed through my thoughts. I reached out and grabbed Linda's arm to steady myself. She was saying something to me, but I couldn't hear her. All I could think about were the images in my head. Jack was in the kennel, on his knees, a horrified look on his face. In an instant, he fell face down, a knife jutting from where it had been planted between his shoulders. Behind him, in the shadows I could see a figure from the waist down, I assumed it was a small dog's perspective.

I felt Linda shaking me. "What?" I managed at last.

"Did you see something?" she asked me.

I nodded and shook my head slowly trying to make sense of what I had seen. "I couldn't see the killer's face, but I—" My words trailed off as Piper was suddenly at my ankles, jumping up, begging to be touched. I scooped her up into my arms and pressed my lips to the top of her head. "Thank you girl; you did a good job."

"What did you see?" Linda asked more adamantly, nearly ready to jump out of her skin.

"I saw a red scarf," I announced. "The killer was wearing a red scarf."

"Seriously?" Linda scoffed.

I shook my head in confusion before giving Piper another quick kiss for a job well done. "Yeah, why?"

"A red scarf? That's the clue that's going to break this case wide open," she wasn't hiding her sarcasm.

"I don't know what you were expecting Linda, they're dogs. It's all they saw."

"Well, that's no help at all," she grumbled. "I guess Mac Murdock it is."

I blew out a breath I hadn't realized I had been holding in. This had all the signs of a disaster waiting to happen. She would simply have to listen to the voice of reason. Before I could say a word, she had started up again.

"We'll take the dogs back and feed them, then we can head over to Mac's," Linda explained before she grunted, bending in half to start calling the dogs over to their leashes. "That Chinese Crested mix sure is a stubborn one, isn't she?"

"Grace? Reminds me of someone else I know."

"I am not stubborn!" she disagreed. "We're just going over to talk to a member of our community and check in on him. I am sure he's rattled to learn a fellow dog catcher's life was ended in such a tragic way. He probably needs a shoulder to lean on right now anyway."

I sucked in a deep breath and then pressed two fingers to my neck, exaggerating finding my pulse and exhaled. "Yeah, it's official, you're going to be the death of me."

"Come on drama llama. Let's get these dogs back; we have a man to comfort."

"Are you insane? We can't go around asking the people in Wyoming if they killed Jack."

Linda chuckled. "Please, give me more credit, I think I can do better than just flat out asking him. Besides, I never said he was the killer for certain. He's just the first lead."

"Lead? Oh, I don't have a good feeling about this," I protested, placing Piper back down onto the ground gently.

"Why would you? There's an excellent chance you were Mac Murdock's target."

I gasped, exasperated by the conversation. "Will you stop it already? Mac Murdock isn't the killer," I proclaimed firmly, confident in my assessment of the seventy-four-year-old, occasionally spacey, but overall pleasant man.

"We shall see, won't we," Linda practically fluttered across the grass in excitement as she gathered up the last dogs she had leashed. "Come on, we better get back and feed them before they turn on us."

In that instant, an image of bacon filled my mind. My head jerked in Piper's direction. "Yes, you can eat too," I assured her as I started to wrangle the dogs I had walked to the park.

"By the way Linda, Grace is looking for a forever home if—"

"If I haven't said yes to the other fifty dogs you've tried to pawn off on me, why on earth would you think that cantankerous old snaggletooth would get me to?"

"Oh," I smiled, "I don't know, cantankerous old things can start to grow on you."

"Real funny," Linda huffed. "We'll see who's laughing when you're wearing stripes."

"They don't wear stripes anymore," I corrected her, trying not to let her prison reference unsettle me.

"Fine, I guess you can let me know if orange is the new black when I come visit you and your new girlfriend Brunhilda on visiting day at the lock up," Linda persisted.

I thought about her words for a moment. "Point taken, let's get back so we can head over to see Mr. Murdock."

～

CHAPTER FOUR

"I HAVE a fitting with Patrice Wellington at four o'clock, so no dilly-dallying," Linda instructed me as she rang the doorbell and straightened out her jumbo print houndstooth coat.

"Me? I didn't even want to come here," I protested, pulling the scarf Linda had knitted for me last Christmas a little tighter around my neck, and securing a few stray strands of my chestnut hair behind my ear.

"Oh, sure you did," Linda brushed off my statement with a wave of her hand. "You, Penny Preston, have never done anything in your life that you didn't want to do."

She had me, I was rather bullheaded, and though I could be talked into some crazy ideas, once I dug my heels in on a decision I could not be swayed. There was no denying it.

I heard some scuffling on the other side of the door and fell quiet as I waited. Finally, Mac Murdock pulled the door open with a smile on his face. A white cat tried to escape, but he quickly scooped it up into his arms and hugged it close to his body. Perhaps he was sprier than I had given him credit for.

"Will you look here Bernice, we must have died," Mr.

Murdock muttered into the cat's ear as he stroked her. A dog catcher with a pet cat, the irony wasn't lost on me.

"Mr. Murdock, are you okay?" I asked.

"I think so. Other than I assume we're in heaven since there are two angels on my doorstep," he replied, a grin spreading across his face.

"Oh, hush it you old flirt," Linda grimaced, swiping at him with her purse. "It's freezing out here, are you gonna invite us in or what?"

"Linda," I hissed a warning at her, but she ignored me.

"I suppose," Mac offered, stepping to one side. "I wasn't expecting guests, so I haven't tidied up at all."

"Be honest, do you tidy up even when you're expecting guests?" Linda asked as we moved through the door and into the living room. I was mortified.

Mac just chuckled in response. "No, I suppose you're right. It's been too long, Linda Louise. How come we never get together anymore?"

"Because you're a sore loser at Bridge," she touted back at him.

"Well, I'll just have to work on that if it will mean getting to see your lovely face more often. And you Ms. Preston," I was a little surprised he knew my name. "I saw quite a commotion down there at the coffee shop this morning; I hope everything's all right."

I nodded in his direction. "Yes, Mr. Murdock, everything's fine." I was trying not to alarm him. Linda had other ideas.

"If you call a dead body fine," Linda scoffed.

"Dead body?" Mac gasped, letting Bernice down onto the ground. The snow-colored cat immediately ran to my legs and began rubbing herself against my ankles. I was sure to get an earful about this as soon as Piper smelled her on me. "What happened?"

"Murder," Linda answered plainly. "That's what happened."

"Linda!" I exclaimed, my shoulders tightening.

"What?" She replied defiantly. "He got a knife in the back. I'd say it's pretty safe to say he was murdered."

Mac chuckled. "Yeah, I'd say so unless whoever it was happened to be a contortionist. Oh, that was rude of me, wasn't it? I shouldn't joke about the dead. Who did you say it was?" Mac stepped into the living room, closing the gap between us.

"We didn't," Linda grumbled. She narrowed her brow in suspicion. "Don't you already know?"

He shook his head in the negative, "I hear a good bit of the town gossip from my neighbor Ms. Shaw, but I haven't heard anything about this yet."

"So you're telling us that you don't have an ax to grind with Jack Egerton?" Linda replied, her eyes reminding me of a cunning predator.

"Jack? Is that who they found in your shop?" Mac asked, directing his gaze at me. "Oh, that poor boy." I'm not sure if I would have called him a boy. I would estimate Jack to be in his late twenties.

"Where were you last night?" Linda pressed.

"Huh? What crazy are you talking about?" Mac muttered.

"Please, just ignore her," I pleaded. "We were just curious since you were once the dog catcher if maybe you could help us think of any enemies Jack may have had."

Mac chuckled. "Dog catchers don't have many enemies, sweetheart. At least they didn't in my day."

"Are you saying things changed since Jack took over?" Linda pressed.

"Well, no. I never said anything like that. I'd say whoever did old Jackie boy in was mighty angry at some pickle of a mess the kid got himself into."

"So he got into a lot of trouble?" Linda inquired, leaning in and practically drooling as if she were about to devour a porterhouse steak.

Mac shrugged. "I know when he won the election there were a few townspeople who were worried if he was responsible enough for the position. He seemed to be doing an excellent job though as far as I could tell."

"No bitterness about that?" Linda prodded.

Mac laughed again, clearly tickled by Linda's questions. "Why on earth would I be bitter? These old bones were tired. I was happy to do the job as long as the town wanted me, but I'd qualified for retirement years ago. I was thrilled to death when the boy won."

"I see," Linda grumbled, the disappointment heavy in her voice.

"Thank you, Mr. Murdock," I added, reaching out to shake his hand. "We appreciate your time."

"Sure thing Penny, I hope they catch the guy. Such a shame to think something like that could happen in a town like ours." Mac said as he showed us to the door. "And by the way Linda, if you're free for dinner, tonight is spaghetti special down at the diner."

Linda's jaw dropped, and I couldn't help but grin. "I-I'll be washing my hair," she stammered at last.

He smiled at her, took her hand into his, and pressed his lips against the back of her gloved fingers. "Maybe next time," he had added before we left.

Once the door was closed and we were on the other side I laughed out loud.

"Did you hear what that old goat said to me?" Linda asked

"I sure did," I grinned.

"Oh, hush it you, before I tell Deputy Handsome what you really think of him," Linda warned, marching herself down the sidewalk.

"I don't know what you're talking about."

"Go ahead, press your luck," she hissed.

I tightened my lips against one another and buried my face in my scarf as the blustery wind came and momentarily stole my breath away. Mac Murdock clearly was not the killer, and while we may have been one step closer to finding Linda a date, we were nowhere on figuring out who killed Jack Egerton.

~

CHAPTER FIVE

BEING ALONE in the Coffee shop— technically, I wasn't alone since Piper was with me—had never bothered me until now. It's hard to imagine that just twelve hours ago I discovered a dead body on the floor of the kennel.

I kneaded the dough for the cinnamon rolls into pillowy round balls before rolling them out to place the layer of cinnamon and spices on top. I probably had enough banana bread for the morning, but I assumed we might have increased traffic due to the gossip, surely spreading around town. People would want to see where the murder had occurred. They would want to listen for any juicy bits and pieces of the story to share with their neighbors. It was part of being in a small town. The least I could do was make sure they were fed.

Linda had left to meet up with her evening fitting appointments. The evening hours, after most people were off work, were the most common times for Linda to be booked which made her a fantastic volunteer at the kennel. I wished she could have sat with me this evening, while I was still a little—

I screamed, jumping as I heard a tap on the front door. I squinted and could see it was Deputy Hanson. *What is he doing here?* I thought to myself, though secretly I was relieved.

I scurried to the door, Piper staying only a couple of steps away from me the entire time. I am sure she fancied herself a guard dog. Though considering her abnormally short one-and-a-half-inch leg length, she couldn't guard me against much more than a field mouse. Nonetheless, she always tried her best.

"Deputy Hanson," I smiled as I opened the door and he stepped inside. I secured the lock after him and moved into the warmth of the shop. "What are you doing here?"

"I saw your light on, and I thought I would come in and check on you," he answered, following as I moved back to my waiting dough. He sat across from me at the counter. Remembering he was still wearing his stocking cap he quickly pulled it off and ran his fingers through his dark hair.

"That was very sweet of you, but there was no need. As you can see I'm completely fine," I lied through my teeth.

"Good, I'm glad to hear it," he added awkwardly. He was hiding something. Had they found a break in the case?

"That wasn't the only reason you came here tonight, was it?" I asked, studying his face.

His eyes shifted down to the counter and then back to me. His mouth turned into a frown.

"You know very well I am not letting you out of here Derrick Hanson until you tell me what it is that has you all tied up in knots." I narrowed my eyes at him.

"What?" He huffed. "What are you—"

"Deputy," I pressed in a high-pitched tone.

"Fine. The Sheriff wanted to come himself, but I thought you'd do better hearing it from me," he started before hesitating again.

"Hear what from you?" I snapped, not hiding my frustration. "Spit it out. You have me in an outright panic now."

"Oh, no. It's nothing like that. It's just—well, I know you meant well," my stomach sank as soon as I heard him say the words. "But interfering in police business is a crime."

"Interfering?" I gasped, trying to act as though I had no idea what he was talking about. I took a step back and focused my eyes on rolling up and slicing my cinnamon rolls. Wrinkling my nose, I asked, "What on Earth are you talking about?"

"Oh, come on Penny, don't make me say all this," he groaned.

"I see, it's Penny now."

"Fine," he huffed. "Ms. Preston," he continued, exaggerating my name as he did. "Mac called the Sheriff and told us what shenanigans you and Linda were up to."

"He complained?" My mouth dropped open in shock.

"No, not exactly. He said he heard about Jack's death from you and Ms. Louise. He was calling to see if there was something he could do to help."

"I see, so he was doing what any good community member would do. Can you explain to me when checking in on a neighbor became a crime?" There was something about the way that he looked at me that made me wish I had just apologized and told him I would keep my nose out of places it didn't belong. Unfortunately, it was the bull-headed part of me that grabbed hold of my tongue and wouldn't shut up.

I dramatically flounced back against the counter. "I mean Linda and I were worried about how the news would affect our previous, elderly dog catcher, but fine, if you don't want me even talking to other townspeople while you all are investigating this crime—a crime of which I am a victim as well, might I remind you—then I might as well close up shop.

Hopefully, you can solve it before The Half Day Coffeehouse goes under."

"Now stop it right there," his voice sounded frustrated. "You're taking what I said too far, and you know it."

"I know nothing of the sort," I argued shaking my head, my nostrils flared.

He leveled his gaze on me. "People in this town appreciate what you do running not only this coffeehouse but the dog shelter too. Nobody, especially me and Sheriff Wright, want to see you close up shop."

"Is that right?" I asked, crossing my arms. "You appreciate what I do with the shelter, huh?"

He nodded in the affirmative, lifting his brows as he answered, "Of course. I hate to think of what would happen to all of those poor animals if you weren't here to help them find homes."

Handsome and an animal lover, perhaps I had been too hard on Deputy Hanson all these years. After my divorce and moving across the country I had sworn off men, but even I had to admit, only having Piper as a companion could get rather lonely.

"I love hearing you say that because I've got a Puggle named Muggle with your name written all over it," I squealed, wiping my hands on my apron before heading toward the kennel door.

"What? No wait, I didn't say I could—" I could hear the panic in his voice as his words trailed off.

I swallowed hard; I knew what was about to come next. Excuses. Oh, he loved dogs, but he just didn't have room in his life for one. "Yeah, yeah, save it."

"No, actually, I would take him, but I already have three very bossy cats at home," he explained, moving closer to me.

"I never pictured you as a cat man," I answered scrunching my nose.

"I would love to give Muggle a home, but I'm afraid my three ladies are currently ruling the roost," he smiled.

I nodded. "I understand." That was a lie. I could never understand how someone could look an adorable and homeless pup in the eye and tell them they couldn't come home with them. I wasn't done with Deputy Handsome yet, though, I would work on him and his cats opening up to Muggle.

"Well, I better get," he continued. I was still nervous to be alone and wanted to tell him he could stay. To say to him that I, in fact, had a lovely sofa he could sleep on if he felt so inclined to do so. But I just nodded instead. "Remember what we talked about." He added, which irritated me.

"Oh, I'll remember," but I'm not sure if I will follow your rules, I thought to myself. Deputy Hanson just needed to feel like I heard him, he didn't need to know that I had no intention of letting this murder go unsolved. The more I thought about it, the angrier it made me that someone broke into my shop and forever traumatized the dogs in my care. Deputy Hanson would just have to find the killer quick or deal with Linda and me being on the case.

"Are you sure you're going to be all right?" he asked as I followed him to the door.

"Who me?" I waved my hand gesturing I was fine. I wasn't being honest, but I hoped my bravado hid my fear. "I'll be fine." I was desperate for him to say something, anything to keep the conversation going, anything that would keep him here a minute longer and me not alone in an empty building, with a possible killer stalking me.

"Well, goodnight then," he said, offering a tight-lipped smile, and then he stepped out into the brisk cold air. And there I was, alone again ... with Piper and my buns.

～

CHAPTER SIX

When I got up in the morning, I was in a much better mood than I was when I had first arrived home. There was a message on my machine from Linda telling me that she had tracked down the name of Jack's girlfriend and after the coffee shop closed she thought we could pop over and visit her where she worked, at the local real estate office. Despite Deputy Hanson's warning, the idea had me intrigued.

When I arrived at the coffee shop, I decided to go through the rear entrance when I saw the news van parked outside. I assumed since I wasn't around yesterday for them to question me, they decided to try again today. I had entered through the door very slowly, half expecting to see another dead body on the floor in front of me.

Just as I knew it would my presence awakened the dogs who decided my being there must clearly mean it was time to be walked and then fed. Luckily with the full batch of banana bread waiting for me inside and the cinnamon rolls ready to pop into the oven, I had time to do just that.

I took care of getting the rolls in the oven and then it was straight onto pup duty. I was careful to use the alleyway and avoid being seen by the news van. After everyone was walked, and fed I started brewing the coffee and noticed something I had never seen before. Every morning I open promptly at seven a.m. I do this for the commuters who pop in for their daily cup of morning Joe and pastry on their way to work. It was only 6:45 a.m. and already a line was forming and wrapping around the block. Occasionally I may have a person or two five minutes before seven, but nothing like what I was seeing.

I picked up the phone and quickly called Linda. "Please tell me you can help me at the coffee shop today."

"You've got me until 10:30 a.m., and then I have a fitting with the mayor. Apparently, she needs more pantsuits. Who knew, twelve isn't enough."

"Can you ever have too many many suits?" I joked.

"Yes ... yes, you can. And that woman has more than met her quota." Linda answered before hanging up the phone.

Linda was there within five minutes of me unlocking the front door. Mostly people were chattering amongst each other about what had transpired the day before, but every once in a while, one brave patron would have the courage to ask me if it was gruesome, or did I see it happen. After the reporters realized they weren't getting much out of me besides the daily specials even they packed up and called it a day.

Linda stayed until her appointment. I thanked her, and then it was just me with the stream of locals, and some less than local people driving in from the city to see where the dog catcher had been murdered. Based on some stares I received I can say with confidence that some had decided I was involved.

The hours flew by, and despite closing at 1 p.m., I had to stay open until 1:30 to ring out every last customer. The extra pastries I thought I had were cleaned out, and I even sold off the last of my store bought muffins that I had purchased and frozen when my oven broke a few months back.

I knocked on the upstairs door of Linda's seamstress shop and waited. When the door opened, I couldn't help but snicker when I was greeted by Linda in what I can only describe as a Sherlock Holmes-esque hat and a capelet made from Linda's signature black and white large print houndstooth fabric.

"What do you think? I worked on it all night," she panted in excitement.

"I think you have finally gone around the bend," I laughed.

"You'll see, this outfit will inspire confidence."

"Or inspire them to put you away in a rubber room."

"Funny," she snarled, pushing past me, pulling the door to her shop closed and securing the lock.

"Oh, come on. I'm just messing with you," I assured her as she hurriedly moved down the steps in front of me.

"Just get in the car," she huffed. Linda drove exactly what you would expect when looking at her. A powder blue convertible Beetle with a cream-colored top. If the weather were above fifty-five degrees, you could bet that top was down; she'd have on three coats if needed.

"So who is this girl?" I asked as we waited for the car to heat up.

"Her name is Dara Mavin, and she works at Riddle and Hittle Real Estate," Linda continued.

"Wait, Polly Hittle's firm?" Polly Hittle had been one of the first friends I had made after moving here as an adult. She was driven, that much was certain. I heard she once sold someone's house before they even knew they wanted to sell it and the buyers she found weren't looking either. Or then there's the story where she closed a baker's dozen worth of sales in one day.

"Yeah, that's the one," Linda confirmed. "Dara's the office manager." A silence lingered in the car for a moment as I mulled over the fact I was once again heading out with Linda to play detective, despite Deputy Hanson's warning. "Isn't this fun?"

"Isn't what fun?"

"You, me, on the case," Linda replied, as she glanced over and smiled in my direction.

"It would be a lot more fun if I weren't a suspect in a murder investigation," I added, hoping to remind my friend that my life was hanging in the balance.

"Oh, they can't consider you a suspect," Linda chuffed. "I mean, who would ever think you were capable of killing anything."

I watched the street ahead as Linda swerved excessively to avoid a plastic bag in the middle of the road. The person in the oncoming lane honked at her repeatedly causing Linda to smile obnoxiously at the driver.

"I think you might be surprised who thinks of me as a suspect. Deputy Hanson came by to see me last night," I explained.

"Oh, yeah," she made a swooning high pitched noise with her voice.

"It wasn't like that," I quickly corrected her. "He came by to warn me to keep my nose out of the case. Since I'm a suspect and all it could look like I'm trying to interfere with a police investigation."

"That's ridiculous," Linda dismissed. "Deputy Handsome has the hots for you as much as you have for him and he's just telling you that because he's trying to keep you safe. It's sweet when you think about it."

I rolled my eyes. "Listen, nothing is going on between myself and the Deputy."

"Yet," Linda interjected.

"Ever," I confirmed firmly. "He's a cat man, and I'm a dog woman. You know what they say about fighting like cats and dogs."

She shrugged and waved a hand dismissively in my direction before returning it to the wheel. "Pish-posh, that's a bunch of hogwash. Plenty of cats and dogs cohabitate just fine."

"I think we're getting severely derailed here," I interjected, trying to steer the conversation back to one of a sane person. "My point is if we don't figure out who killed Jack soon I could be looking at some serious trouble."

"His girlfriend has to know something," Linda attempted to reassure me, pulling into the parking lot of the cozy cottage looking office. It suited a small town real estate firm perfectly, and I could even imagine it painted on postcards. Heck, knowing Polly Hittle, her office was painted on postcards with a snowy scene and sent out as Christmas cards.

"Why does she think we want to see her?" I inquired, probably a little later than I should have.

Linda didn't answer me as she placed the car in park and opened the door. She stepped out into the cold air, leaned down and quickly stated, "She thinks you want to buy a house," before she closed the door.

"What?" I gasped, but the door closed before I could get the word out. Shoving my door open, I chased after Linda, up the flagstone path and to the red door with black iron trim. "I'm looking to buy what?" I whispered.

"It'll be fine, let me do the talking," Linda replied as she reached out and turned the knob.

"What if Polly sees me, we're friends ya know," I reminded her.

Linda shook her head. "What do you think I'm an amateur or something?"

"Well, yes, now that you ask, I do."

"I called every realtor in the office, got their schedule, and compared them to figure out when they would all be out showing houses or at closings. I then called Ms. Mavin and told her that was the only time your schedule would permit."

I paused. Processing what Linda just said. "Hey, that's really clever."

"I know, now follow me," Linda instructed as she pushed open the door to the sound of a small bell chime. The plain girl I had seen on the streets many times with Jack Egerton came into the small entry area and greeted us. Her eyes were red and swollen, and I suddenly realized she was mourning Jack. He wasn't just a corpse or an inconvenience; he was a person.

"You must be Ms. Louise and Ms. Preston. Hello, my name is Dara Mavin," Dara said holding her hand out to Linda. We both shook the poor girl's hand. She made small talk as she showed us into a small conference room and we sat across from each other. She got straight to business, pulling out a book of available properties for me to flip through.

"Now you should be aware, I am the office manager but if you see a property that piques your interest we have several licensed realtors who would be happy to show the property to you."

"Wonderful," I lied as I continued to flip through the book of properties. I had no intention of purchasing a home. After moving to Wyoming, I bought the perfect two bedroom Tudor in the town square. It was small, but it had a fenced backyard and was everything Piper and I needed, including low cost, which was hard to find in our little picturesque town.

"I'm sorry, I hope you don't mind my asking, is everything all right dear?" Linda finally broke the silence, and my heart stopped beating for a moment.

"Excuse me?" Dara asked, apparently surprised by the question.

"I'm sorry, I don't mean to pry, but I can't help noticing that your eyes are red as if you've been crying."

"Linda, don't be rude," I scolded.

The girl's lip quivered. "No, she's right. I'm afraid my boyfriend was killed recently."

"Oh, my God. I am so sorry to hear that," I gasped, trying my best to act surprised.

"Oh no, don't be," she gave a snotty snort. "He was a real jerk."

"I see," I grimaced.

"That must sound terrible, I'm so sorry." She continued, shaking her head for a moment. "He was still in love with his ex-girlfriend. I've been crying because now I just found out he's been stealing money out of my bank account. I don't know what I'm going to do." The more I learned about our dearly departed Jack Egerton, the less I seemed to care he was gone.

"Wait, this wasn't by chance the dog catcher, was it?" Linda gasped as if the revelation had surprised her somehow.

"You knew him?" Dara asked, a confused look puzzling its way across her face.

"Oh, honey. I'm so sorry. Ms. Preston here was the one that found him." Linda continued. My jaw dropped in utter shock as I realized Linda had just figuratively thrown me under the bus.

Dara's eyes fixed on me, her brows lowering, "You what? You're the one that owns that kennel?"

"Y-Yes." I stuttered.

Her fists tightened into white-knuckled balls. "Great, then can you tell me what the heck Jack was doing there? Were the two of you—having an affair?"

I winced at the suggestion. "Oh God, no."

"Then why was he there?" She demanded, standing and pulling the book away from my hands.

"I wish I knew," I said in an almost whisper.

She swallowed hard and averted her eyes away from both Linda and me. I felt so ashamed that I had could have ever thought that this was a good idea. If I were honest, though, Linda wasn't to blame. I was so eager to figure out who could have done this to everyone's lives that it didn't take much coaxing to get me here.

"I think you two should go," she stated in a flat tone.

"Of course," I answered, and stood. "I am so sorry."

"You didn't see any properties you liked?" Linda asked me before standing as well. Leave it to her to stick with even a bad con until the end.

Through gritted teeth I growled, and gripped Linda by the arm, pulling her along. "Now is clearly a bad time, we should go."

"Wait a second," Linda stopped cold in her tracks and pulled her arm out of my grasp. She looked Dara square in the eyes and said, "I'm sorry to hear about your boyfriend. I'm sorry to hear that when he was alive, he treated you so badly. You seem like a lovely girl, and that's not fair. My friend here is a beautiful girl too, and if they can't figure out who killed your boyfriend, they could start looking at her for it."

Dara shook her head. "What's your point?"

"Just if you think of anything that might help us find the real killer, we'd appreciate a call." I couldn't believe the moxie of this woman. I didn't know if I should cry or kiss her.

"Get out," Dara replied in a cold voice, her eyes fixed on me.

"Of course, we're so sorry to have bothered you," I added before turning and literally dragging Linda out of the cozy white cottage. All I could think was that the next call I would get would either be from Polly asking me what I was thinking coming and upsetting her employee the way I did or from Deputy Hanson to let me know they would be by shortly to arrest me for interfering with a police investigation.

When we were outside the front door, Linda huffed in frustration. "She was about to crack, I know it."

"What are you talking about?" I exclaimed, throwing my arms up into the air. "This isn't one of your crime novels; this is people's lives we're dealing with."

"I know that," Linda squeaked, her eyes grew wide and glistened. "I'm doing this for you."

"Are you?" I quipped, turning and getting into the passenger side of the Beetle.

A moment later she joined me. "I'm sorry, I—"

"Just take me back to Half Day, please." I requested. We rode the entire trip in silence. There were several times I could tell that Linda wanted to say something, but I would shift, turning my body as far away from her as I could, and she would close her mouth again.

She said goodbye as we were getting out of the car, but I had nothing for her. After what I had just put that poor grieving girl through, I had nothing left at all. All I wanted to do was go inside and spend some time with the dogs, the only living beings I should probably ever be allowed to be around.

As soon as I walked through the back door, Piper made her way from her pillow bed, an image of a heart relayed to me through her thoughts, quickly followed by a plate of biscuits and sausage gravy.

～

CHAPTER SEVEN

"BACON, I get it, Piper. You're just going to have to be patient," I snapped, my head jerking in the direction of the round, ground-hugging, Dachshund near my feet. I'd overslept due to a night filled with tossing and turning over my argument with Linda. I had entered into this crazy plan to become pretend detectives willingly and knowingly. Linda had not deserved my wrath as much as Dara Mavin had not deserved our invading her time of grief. I needed to apologize.

The line at the coffeehouse had been just as long around the block today as it had been yesterday when I opened the little shop. I assumed everyone was out in hopes of catching a glimpse of me, the crazy coffeehouse killer. At least, that's what it seemed like by the way they looked at me when they ordered.

My breath caught in my throat when Deputy Hanson walked up to the counter. I can't say that I was surprised. If I were Dara Mavin, the first thing I would have done when Linda and I left would have been to call the police and file a complaint.

To my shock, he only offered a soft smile and asked, "What do you have coming out of that oven today?"

My stomach had fluttered before I answered and I had to force the words free. "I'm sorry to say it's banana bread again."

He chuckled. "Never be sorry for your banana bread. I'll take a slice and coffee with cream no sugar."

My mouth fell open for a moment. Had Dara Mavin not called the police? Based on the softness of Derrick's eyes it appeared she had not.

"I can grab the bread if you want to pour the coffee." My head snapped up in response to Linda's voice behind me. I spun around and looked at the shorter gray-haired woman as she tied an apron around her waist.

"W-what are you doing here?" I stammered.

"Are you kidding, that line's a mile long. If I don't help you people will never be able to get in and out of the parking lot to get to my shop," she huffed. I knew this was a lie because Linda Louise had always had a strict by appointment only policy. It was not only written on the sign over her shop, but it was also on her business cards, and in fine print on her logo.

I smiled and mouthed the words thank you.

"Well, are you going to stand there all day or are you going to get to work so we can get these looky loos out of here?" Linda chimed, as she shrugged her shoulders, then proceeded to bag up a slice of my banana bread.

"I'm so—" I started to apologize before Linda interrupted me.

"Coffee," she reminded me as she offered a fleeting smile, I assumed to let me know yesterday was already long forgotten.

"You have some pretty great tenants," Deputy Hanson

said as he watched the two of us interact. "It must be nice to have a friend close by to help out whenever you need."

"Or secretly it's my path to rent control. As long as she can't live without me my rent should never go up," Linda snickered as she passed the Deputy the bag and took his money to the register.

Linda grew up near Wyoming. Most people here either grew up here or nearby. It was almost like Wyoming was straight out of a fifty's family sitcom, but Linda didn't fit the mold. She wasn't born into wealth, and she wasn't married to a CEO of some big company in the nearby major city, Cincinnati. She married her high school sweetheart, and when he passed away ten years ago, she decided the best cure for a heartache was a great mystery novel. I couldn't imagine running the animal rescue without her help. One month I wasn't sure how I was going to make enough to cover the cost of the food. But Linda pulled through with a fundraiser where she sewed dog coats and hats out of scrap fabric she had at a table on the sidewalk in front of the coffee shop. It was enough to keep us going for another six months and helped the kennel through a rough patch.

You could never tell her thank you, though. She was humble and would always come up with an excuse as to why she was helping you, never willing to admit, in fact, what a kindhearted woman she was. On Thursdays, she played bridge at the local retirement home, something she had done since her early forties. She would rarely let them win, but if one were having a bad day, it often would just happen to be the day they finally were able to beat her.

The line of people continued to stream in and out of the shop until every last slice of banana bread was gone; I was left with selling coffee for the last hour of the day.

"Well, I guess one good thing came out of me being a suspected killer, I haven't been this busy since ... well, ever."

As soon as I said the words, I realized how bad they sounded. "Not that I'm happy for one second that a man's life was—"

Linda raised a hand and smiled, "I know what you meant."

"Bacon!" I exclaimed as I remembered Piper's repeated desperate attempts to communicate with me. My eyes searched the ground until I caught sight of my red-haired beauty on the oversized pillow under the counter. She had given up and decided sleep may help calm the hunger pains.

"Hungry?" Linda asked with raised eyebrows.

I shook my head, a sullen frown on my face. "No, just realizing what a bad mom I would be. Piper has been telling me all morning she was hungry."

She laughed. "I wouldn't feel too bad if I were you. To me, it looks like the old girl could stand to miss a few meals."

"She's slimmed down quite a bit," I quickly defended my kindred spirit pet. "I can see some definition around where her back legs meet her body."

"Oh, yeah. She's a regular Jane Fonda," Linda scoffed, as she walked around the counter and locked the door behind the last straggling customers.

"Thanks for today," I added as I pulled the pre-cooked bacon out of the box and microwaved a slice. Piper loved when I crumbled it up on her dry dog food. However, this was not a necessity to get her to eat the food. If there were any food within her reach, it would be eaten.

"Don't mention it," Linda replied, walking back to the counter and taking a seat opposite me. "If this becomes the norm, though, you may have to think about hiring someone."

I shook my head. "This will fade," I assured her. "You know how it is; I'm just today's gossip."

"You're probably right, but wedding season is around the corner which means I will be swamped at the shop. I can help with the dogs whenever it's possible, but I won't be able to bail you out here when I'm busy."

"Here you go," I say as I set down Piper's bowl in front of her. She was awake from the moment I opened the bacon wrapper, eagerly anticipating her meal. The image of a heart flashed through my mind, and though Piper was already scarfing down her food, I knew that was her way of saying thank you.

"If it's still like this after two weeks then maybe I will look for someone. I would hate to bring someone in only to have to turn around and let them go again."

Linda arched an eyebrow in my direction. "Always the one to be thinking about others, aren't you?"

I shrugged. Compliments had always made me uncomfortable. I knew who I was and I liked myself just fine, I didn't need other's telling me, even if it was just their way of being nice.

As soon as I took a sip of my now room temperature coffee that had been waiting for me on the counter since I poured it three customers ago, Linda said something that made me spray my drink halfway across the room. "I called Dara Mavin last night."

"You what?" I gasped before coughing repeatedly.

Linda waved her hands in my direction and shook her head. "Calm down, before you get your panties knotted, let me explain."

"Oh, this better be good."

"I wanted to make sure she wasn't going to run off to Sheriff Wright after the warning Deputy Hanson gave you."

"So you decided it would be a good idea to call and harass her some more?"

Linda drew in a sharp breath. "It wasn't like that! I told her that you really liked one of the houses you saw in the book she showed you."

"Linda!" I exclaimed. "I have a house, I don't want to buy another one."

"I know. I know. But I needed something to lead with. I just didn't want you to be surprised if she followed up with you at some point on that. Did you know she's working toward becoming a realtor? She's a very sweet girl."

"Get to the point," I huffed, not hiding my frustration.

"You're going to be glad I did call her when you find out what we talked about. She was asking about you and Jack—"

"She what?"

"Yeah, I still don't think she was convinced there wasn't some kind of hanky panky going on," Linda snickered.

"I hope you set her straight," I yelped.

"Of course," She huffed. "I also explained how upset you were over finding Jack's body the way you did and how it just devastated you when you heard that he had a girlfriend that he left behind—"

"It did?" I narrowed my eyes.

"Yes, it did. I know you better than you know yourself, and I say it did." Linda barked back before continuing her story. "Anyways, I told her that you were determined to find the killer not just because he or she could be after you next, but you wanted to do it for her and Jack."

"What did she say?" I asked, hanging on Linda's every word.

"She said you should probably save your sympathy for someone other than Jack because he was the last person that deserved it."

"No!" I gasped, leaning in for the juicy bits. "She was pretty ticked about him stealing her money wasn't she?"

"Oh, it goes deeper than that. Dara told me that she had been trying to break up with Jack for months because it was obvious that he was still in love with his ex and that no matter how hard she tried he just wouldn't go away. He was like some gum that would get stuck to the bottom of your shoe, and you couldn't get off no matter how hard you tried."

"If he was in love with his ex then why would he fight so hard for Dara not to break up with him?" I asked with a puzzled look on my face.

"That's the million-dollar question, isn't it?" Linda chimed.

I shook my head, "It doesn't make sense. Is she lying? Do you think she could have—" I started, my mouth now hanging open.

"I know where you're going with this and she doesn't strike me as a killer," Linda replied. "However, she did give me some very helpful information."

I stared at her, my lips parted and my eyes wide. Linda wasn't saying anything. "Well?" I blurted out at last, desperate to know exactly what Dara had revealed.

"So you remember she said she suspected that Jack was having an affair with his ex-girlfriend and had been for quite some time. That was why she had been trying to break up with him, and she couldn't figure out why he kept begging her not to leave him. After she saw the bank statements and realized Jack was stealing from her it all made sense. Isn't it great?"

"Isn't what great?"

"We have our next lead," Linda grinned.

"Okay wait, I'm confused. We what?"

"Have you met Brik Ford?"

"He's been in a few times." Brik Ford had a reputation for having his hands in everything illegal around these parts. If there was a black market for an item, Brik was your man. He was also dumb as a box of rocks. I mean seriously, I doubt if he would even be able to land a job as a taster in a pie making factory. "Why?"

"Dara told me that when she started to think Jack was cheating she did a little digging, she found out that Jack's ex was dating Brik Ford."

"And?" I breathed, repeatedly blinking.

"And we need to go talk to him," Linda added plainly.

"Slow down," I pleaded, waving my hands. "You've lost me."

"Dara gave me two possible motives for what happened to Jack," Linda explained.

"I bet she did," I huffed, blowing my bangs up off my forehead for a moment. "Did it ever cross your mind that Dara is just trying to shift suspicion off of her because she's the one that killed Jack? I mean, if she has suspects, why not go to the Sheriff with that information."

"For that exact reason," Linda answered excitedly. "She has motive, and she knows it. She's afraid if she tells the Sheriff anything he'll figure that out."

"Maybe the Sheriff should know," I suggested.

Linda waved her hands, "Just hear me out." She pleaded. "Dara made some good points. What if Jack was secretly back with his ex-girlfriend and this was all a sham? What if they were both secretly stealing from their significant others?"

"From what I've heard about Brik Ford that probably wouldn't bode well for either of them," I replied.

"Maybe the ex wasn't in on it, but Brik Ford has a reputation where even the rumor of Jack sleeping with his girl would send him over the edge," Linda pointed out.

I stumbled back a couple of steps and stiffened my back as I stood upright. "Which is why we need to go straight to the Sheriff with this."

"Are you done?" she huffed, crossing her arms. "That's all just a bunch of gossip. Brik might be a thief, but he's no killer. I mean he might be a murderer if he killed Jack, but it's not like he kills people on a regular basis."

"You are not making me feel any better," I cried.

"I promise," Linda attempted to reassure me. "We're just going to go talk to him. We will be very careful what we say."

A flash of a big red stop sign raced through my thoughts. I looked down to see Piper wide-eyed staring up at me; even she thought this was an insane idea. "I know girl; we'll be careful. There's nothing to worry about." I hoped I wasn't lying to Piper.

～

CHAPTER EIGHT

I SIGHED as we sat in Linda's powder blue Beetle, staring up the long snow-covered drive. I remember driving past the Ford family property when I was a kid, and imagining that the big house on top of the hill must have belonged to someone rich and famous. At the time, it had been Brik's father who owned the home, and while he wasn't famous, there was no doubt he was rich.

Brik's dad had been a lawyer and a senator at one time. He was an intellectual and a well-respected member of the community. When he and his wife retired to Arizona due to Mr. Ford's severe allergies, they left the family home to Brik. Besides my rare interactions with him at the coffeehouse, this had been the extent of my knowledge of him—besides town gossip.

Considering that Brik had never been the sharpest tool in the shed, and he had no job that would provide the amount of income needed to maintain the property taxes on such a considerable sized estate, rumors swirled. He had a long trail of failed businesses including landscaping where people of the town paid months in advance for services that few received.

"You know what I heard?" Linda asked as she stared up the long drive as well. "I heard he grows and sells pot."

"No, he doesn't!" I exclaimed.

Linda shook her head, "I'm just telling you what I heard." Linda heard an incredible amount of gossip around Wyoming. My guess is it had a lot to do with who the members were of her murder mystery book club. There was Mrs. Shaw, the town librarian who knew more shady things about people than their local bartender. Then, of course, there was the Sheriff's wife, June Wright. Even though she was the sweetest lady you would ever meet, the juicy things she would hear listening in on her husband's work always seemed to slip out on book club night.

"Should we go up?" I inquired, wondering how long we had been sitting there in silence.

"I've been practicing what to say in my head," Linda replied.

"I suppose that's better than just winging it," I said and then began to snicker as I processed just how ridiculous we both were being. "What are we doing?"

"What do you mean?" Linda asked with a puzzled look on her face.

"We're not detectives," I started to laugh harder which made Linda angry at first. Before long, she started laughing too.

"This is a little crazy, isn't it?" I nodded in response to her question. "We should probably just go back to the—"

Before Linda could finish her statement, there was a knock on her window, and we both screamed in surprise. Standing before us was Brik Ford in his big heavy coat. We had been so engrossed in our conversation that we hadn't noticed Brik's truck pull up behind us in the drive.

"What do I say?" Linda asked in a panic.

"I don't know, make something up," I instructed her, my heart now racing.

She pressed the small button to her left, and I watched in horror as the window lowered. I had images of a gun coming out of his pocket with a silencer on the tip, and him pointing it directly at us. I reminded myself that I needed to get a grip.

"H-hi." Linda stammered. "I'm sorry, are we blocking your driveway? If you back up we can get out of your way."

Brik ignored her and instead crouched lower so he could see who was in the passenger seat. Brik had long curly, frizzy sandy blonde hair, a trait he received from his mother, that he wore pulled back in a ponytail. I don't think I had ever seen him without a five o'clock shadow, which I assumed must be quite a feat because how do you keep it trimmed so close without ever being seen completely clean shaven. Though, considering I had had facial hair all of zero days in my life I assumed this could all be a fundamental lack of understanding of how facial hair works in the first place.

His eyes narrowed and then widened in what I assumed was recognition, "Penny Preston," he chimed knowingly in a sing-song voice, and I was surprised he knew who I was.

"That's me," I shrugged, forcing a smile on my face.

"What are you doing here?" Brik asked.

"Oh nothing," I replied, no idea what would possibly be a believable excuse for us to be waiting at the end of his driveway.

"Is that right?" he followed up. The puzzled look on my face must have told him I had no idea what in the heck he was talking about. "Were you the one who found Jack Egerton's body?"

My stomach sank. Brik Ford may have never given who I was a second thought before I became the girl that discovered the body of the dog catcher. Through a tight-lipped smile, I replied, "I'm afraid so."

"Whoa!" he bellowed, "was his head all disconnected like they said?"

"What? No!" I exclaimed. "Is that what they're saying?"

Brik nodded. "Yup, I heard his head was chopped clean off."

"Ick, no! That's terrible," I grumbled.

"Your girlfriend, April, used to date Jack Egerton, didn't she?" Linda asked cooly. I wanted to start shouting abort, to remind her that we had only moments ago made the decision that this was crazy and the last thing that we should be doing.

Brik looked stunned by Linda's question; he stood before he stated, "A snowman could get frostbite out here, why don't you ladies drive on up to the house, and we can talk inside where it's warm."

Brik turned toward his truck before I could voice my protests.

"We're not going up to that house," I announced to Linda.

"He has us blocked in, what am I supposed to do?" Linda asked as she rolled up her window. I looked over my shoulder to see if I could gauge Brik's expression behind the wheel, but the sun glared on the glass of his windshield, obstructing my view.

"Drive up but when we get to the house turn around so we can get back down the drive as soon as he clears it," I ordered.

"Good plan," she agreed.

Linda did as I told her, but much to our dismay Brik parked his oversized black truck just where the bottleneck of the drive ended, forcing us to stay exactly where we were, trapped.

"Come on in," he extended the invitation as he stepped out of the truck and walked to the front door and my mind immediately began evaluating. Was there a sinister tone to the invitation or was it sincere? I couldn't decide, there was too little to go on.

"What do we do?" I asked Linda, the panic now heavy in my whispered voice.

"As long as we don't act like anything is wrong then everything should be fine," Linda answered as she opened her door, but I had little confidence in her logic. "Besides, the ground is frozen; he has to know how hard it would be to bury two bodies this time of year."

I pushed my door open, quickly following her, "Not funny Linda. Not funny!"

She chuckled at my response.

We followed the same path up to the door Brik had left open for us. When I walked into the oversized colonial style home I had expected dark paneling and for some reason black and red decor in every room. Much to my surprise the space was bright and airy. Inside the entryway, there was an antique table where Brik had tossed his keys. I considered grabbing them and flying out to move his truck myself, but knew that would make me seem quite insane, even though I would certainly remain very much alive.

"Can I get you ladies anything to drink? April will be down soon, I'm sure."

"April's here?" I gasped in relief.

Brik furrowed his brow. "Do you two know each other?"

"Uh, no," Linda interjected. "She was just telling me in the car how lovely it would be to officially meet your girlfriend since the word around town is what a beautiful girl she is."

"Yeah, she's pretty great," Brik said as he moved into the large living room that housed two oversized white leather couches. "Drink?" he asked again.

"No thanks." Linda and I responded in harmony.

Brik sat down on one of the couches and motioned for us to join him. He was eyeing Linda. "Do you know my mom?"

"Why because all old ladies know each other?" Linda snarled making her way to the couch across from Brik. I sat next to her and squeezed her arm to remind her that we had no clue who we were dealing with.

Brik laughed, "I like you. So, do you want to tell me why you two were really sitting in my driveway?" Perhaps Brik Ford wasn't as dumb as everyone said he was.

"Excuse me?" I coughed.

"The girl who runs the dog rescue where they found my girlfriend's ex-boyfriend's body shows up at my house. Yeah, I think we both already know why you ladies are here," Brik continued.

"We do?" Linda's voice cracked.

"For the same reason, the Sheriff was out here asking me a bunch of questions yesterday."

"He was?" I asked, somewhat relieved to hear that they were taking the investigation into Jack's murder seriously. After all, how else could I be exonerated unless they figured out who the actual killer was?

"Yes, he was," a woman's voice came from the right. My head turned to find the source, and I caught a glimpse of a beautiful and slender blonde woman as she glided down the staircase.

"Hey babe," Brik called out to her. She moved swiftly, crossing the room. Her denim was dark, and I assumed it must be from a popular label based on the way she looked as though she must be into all the current fashion trends. Sweeping her hair off to one side she sat down next to Brik who watched her with a huge smile planted on his face.

"So you're the one who found Jack?" April asked, eyeing me up and down.

I swallowed hard, uneasy about the way she was examining me. "Yes, I was."

"Did you know him?" she asked.

"Not really, we occasionally crossed paths when I had room to take in some of the strays he came across," I explained.

"Ugh, I will never understand why he even wanted that terrible job," April grumbled as she rolled her eyes with a look of disgust on her face.

"Not a dog lover?" Linda asked.

"Oh no, I have a teacup Chihuahua I adore—"

"It's true, she does," Brik laughed. "The thing looks like a drowned rat, but she loves it just the same."

April playfully slapped Brik with the back of her hand. "She does not," April laughed as she feigned protest. "She's perfect."

"Then what was it about the job that you disapproved of?" I pressed her.

April's eyes fluttered as she recalled. "It became his entire life. Someone was always calling him and telling him they found a stray they wanted him to pick up. It's also not the most lucrative job; I'm not sure you knew that."

"Yeah, not surprising," I replied.

April stifled a laugh.

"What is it?" Brik inquired.

"I was just thinking about the last time we saw Jack," April said, apparently trying to remove the smile that was firmly planted on her face.

Brik nodded. "That had to be a pretty low moment for the guy."

Linda shook her head. "How so? What happened?"

April stood and walked toward a cabinet on the far side of the room, retrieving something from a small box on one of the shelves. She returned and handed a thin banded golden ring to me. I examined it closer, noticing the little diamond on it wasn't much more than a chip.

"I don't understand," I replied, handing her the trinket back.

April snickered as Brik replied for her. "He proposed to her in front of me with that. He went all Romeo on her and then dropped down on one knee."

"What did you do?" Linda asked, clearly enthralled with the story.

April seemed surprised by her question. "Seriously? Did you see the ring?" She cringed as she looked back down at the golden token before returning it to its former hiding place.

"I told him that there was no way he could ever afford to make me happy on a dog catcher's salary," April explained, moving back to sit next to Brik, kissing him on the cheek before she nestled in under his arm. "He wouldn't take the ring back after I told him no. He said he got it for me and he wanted me to keep it. I suggested he give it to that plain girl he was seeing, but that just seemed to make him angry, so I agreed to keep it."

"And you were just okay with him proposing to your girl-friend?" Linda boldly posed the question to Brik.

"I'm secure in our relationship," his eyes sparkled as he spoke. "Besides, if April isn't happy with me then she should go, there are plenty of fish in the sea." *His love for her was over-whelming*, I thought to myself sarcastically. Brik obviously delighted in her beauty, but there was no way he was going to lose any sleep over April and Jack. If Jack and April were having an affair, she should earn an Oscar. Somehow I doubted she was that good of an actress.

"When was this?" Linda asked.

April bit at her lip, looking at Brik, me and then Linda again. She narrowed her eyes. "What's with all these questions?"

"What do you mean?" I asked, hoping to deflect the sudden distrusting attitude.

"I mean, you I get," she nodded in my direction. "You found his body, but what's with the old lady? Why do you want to know?"

I looked at Linda, unsure how to answer the question. I didn't have to. Before either of us could answer Brik stepped in. "Honey, they want to know if we had anything to do with his death."

"We—" I gasped, unsure what to say next. He was right, but I couldn't tell them that. What if he killed Jack? If he thought we suspected him, we could be next.

"They what?" April shot upright, her mouth dropping open.

"We're just trying to fit the pieces together," I insisted. "Nobody's accusing anyone of anything."

"I want them to leave Brik," April crossed her arms and collapsed against the back of the couch.

Brik stood. "You heard the lady. I'll move my truck." I sucked in a sharp breath. He knew exactly what he was doing when he blocked us in his driveway. He was playing us all along. Was he still playing us?

We offered our apologies to April as we exited, but she did not reply. As we were about to get in the car, Brik called after us, "You should talk to his sister."

"Excuse me?" I asked, my eyes fixed on Brik, trying to assess what his possible motive could be in helping us besides throwing us off his scent.

"Jill Egerton, she came here not too long ago looking for Jack, and she was mighty ticked off. I told her that we hadn't seen Jack since the night he proposed, months ago, but she didn't believe me. She warned me that if I were in on it, she would be coming back to see me next." Brik turned away, walking toward his truck.

"In on what?" Linda yelled after him.

"I don't know, she never said." Brik climbed into his truck

and pulled up next to the Beetle. Linda turned the key, flipped on the headlights, and just as flurries began to fall we headed out into the night; the next piece of the puzzle in front of us.

CHAPTER NINE

"I THOUGHT SO!" Linda exclaimed, running into the coffee shop with a ticket in her hand.

"You thought what?" I asked a puzzled look on my face as I mixed batter for blueberry muffins. The secret was waiting until everything was mixed and then gently folding in the blueberries. Otherwise, you could end up with a bunch of smurfily delicious muffins.

"Jill Egerton called me last month about getting alterations for a formal gown she has," Linda explained.

"So you know her?"

"Not exactly," Linda hesitated, scrunching up her face. "I never called her back."

"What?" I growled. "Why on Earth would you have not called her back?"

Linda looked up just in time to catch my look of disappointment. She sighed. "You know how disorganized I am. I tell you all the time how I need an assistant to keep track of things. Do you know how many people need alterations heading into the holiday season?"

"So what? You just want to up and call her out of the blue a month later?" I choked out the question.

She shrugged. "Why not? Seems as good as any other reason to call her."

I leaned against the counter, drinking in the sweet aroma of the blueberry-rich batter. She was right. "Fine, it's worth a try."

There was a knock on the window of the coffeehouse. I squinted toward the night on the other side of the glass and realized it was Sheriff Wright. Linda shoved the pink message slip into her pocket, an uneasy look on her face.

"Just play it cool," I whispered as I moved around the counter and made my way to the door.

I assumed there was no reason for him to be here other than Brik and April reporting our recent visit. I prepared myself for the earful.

"Sheriff Wright, what are you doing here?" I chimed in what I suddenly worried was an overly boisterous voice.

"Do you have a second, Penny?" he inquired, removing his hat to reveal his gray hair as he stepped inside the entrance of the coffeehouse. I locked the door behind him and turned back toward the counter. Careful not to make eye contact with him as we spoke.

"Certainly, I was just getting some pastries ready for the morning rush," I answered, getting ready to pour the blueberry batter into the muffin tins and pop them in the oven. "With all this craziness lately I can never seem to have enough sweet treats on hand for customers, so I've taken to doing an extra batch the night before."

"I see," he rapped his knuckles on the counter.

"Everything all right Willard?" I asked.

"Did Deputy Hanson talk to you?" he asked. And there it was. I was faced with a decision. Based on that question Sheriff Wright already knew what Linda and I had been up to.

"How's June? We all missed her at book club last week," Linda interjected.

"Huh?" he huffed, "Oh, she's fine. Just pulled her back out while she was ... uh, changing the sheets." I knew for a fact this was a lie because our gray-haired darling friend, June Wright, had recently called Linda to explain that she, in fact, had thrown her back out while attempting a move she saw on television called twerking. I decided to spare the Sheriff the embarrassment of knowing that we knew exactly how wild and crazy his wife was.

"I talk to Deputy Hanson all the time, which exact time are you referring to?" I asked, after having another moment to think of how best to respond.

The Sheriff furrowed his brow. "Why do I believe you know exactly what I'm talking about?"

"Uh, well," I hesitated, my eyes darting toward Linda. I shrugged. "Maybe I do know which time you're talking about."

He tilted his head forward as he glared at me from under his droopy brow, "Maybe?"

"Okay, fine," I huffed, accepting the impending lecture. "He told me to quit asking around about Jack Egerton."

"Perhaps I should allow the two of you to discuss this alone," Linda suggested as she prepared to turn and exit the shop through the back. My jaw dropped at her cowardly words.

"Not so fast Linda Louise," Sheriff Wright interjected. "I think perhaps this is a conversation you need to be part of as well, don't you?"

I smiled triumphantly as Linda grimaced and plopped onto the stool beside me with a heavy sigh. A snicker managed to pry its way from me causing Linda to deliver a sharp glance in my direction before swiping the batter-covered spoon from my hand. She proceeded to pick out the random blueberries, popping them into her mouth before waving her hand in the direction of the Sheriff for him to continue.

"Now I can go into a long explanation about how you ladies are interfering with an ongoing investigation. I can also tell you that if there is a killer out there roaming the streets of our tiny town, your questions are going to bring him right to your doorstep," Sheriff Wright warned us.

My brain was telling me that my best course of action here would be to remain silent and let the Sheriff finish his lecture, but my mouth apparently did not agree. "Begging your pardon Willard, the killer has already been at my doorstep. In fact, they were in my shop, the shop that my aunt loved so dearly and entrusted to me, where they decided to take a man's life. I won't apologize for trying to figure out who did this."

"And you won't stop either," the Sheriff breathed slowly with a nod.

"W-what?" Linda stammered.

"What I was trying to tell you is that even though I could go on with a whole list of why you ladies shouldn't be doing what you are," the Sheriff continued, "I know no matter what I say; you'll both continue this insanity."

"So you're going to let us—" I started before he lifted a hand to silence me, effectively cutting me off.

"Now hold on, don't get ahead of yourself." I could see he was trying to keep a serious expression on his face, but when he looked at me, it was hard for him not to smile. "You ladies need to understand, if you break the law in any way, I will be forced to arrest you. I may have known you since you were a little girl Penny Preston and Linda, I golfed with your late husband Earl, but that doesn't mean I can ignore my duties as Sheriff. Got me?"

"Oh, of course," I gasped. "We would never—"

"That includes trespassing or harassing the good citizens of Wyoming, Ohio," he added in an authoritative tone.

Both Linda and I began to shake our heads wildly, and I added, "Absolutely, we promise, we would never—"

"Yes you would," he hissed. "And that's why I'm here. You know my wife and I care about you Penny, but I will do my job. This isn't me approving what you're doing; it's me letting you know that we're watching you."

His threats fell on deaf ears. All I heard was that he understood Linda and I wouldn't quit searching for the killer. He should have just deputized us.

Sheriff Wright reached out, gently gripping my wrist, his eyes widened slightly, and the dim light glinted off his concerned gaze, "I need you to promise me something."

My head tilted in understanding. "Absolutely." I shrugged. "What is it?"

He looked at Linda and then back at me, his hand slipped from my wrist, and he said emphasizing every word, "Promise me if you find something, anything, you'll bring it straight to me."

Linda laughed, before replying in a shrill voice, "You know we will. Do you think we're crazy?"

"Yes, I do. Anyone who goes out looking for a killer who hasn't been properly trained is insane in my book," Sheriff Wright snapped back.

"I promise, we'll come straight to you if we uncover anything that could affect the case. We just want to help," I insisted.

"Well, the guy certainly had no shortage of enemies. It seems like we are discovering someone new that hated him at every turn," he grumbled.

"We have noticed there wasn't a lot of love for him around town," Linda added.

The Sheriff laughed out loud. "Not a lot of love for him?

Goodness, even his sister hated his guts." He shook his head. "I'm getting off topic. All I'm saying is, the killer could be anyone so while I prefer you just stop this nonsense altogether, I at least need you to be smart about it," he said looking directly at me.

I nodded and offered a smile. "I promise."

He drew in a deep breath and started to turn, hesitating for a moment.

"Is there something else?" I asked in a soft voice.

"You wouldn't happen to have any of those blueberry muffins ready now, would you?"

I smiled, reached under the counter and revealed a pre-boxed muffin I had prepared for the morning rush. "On the house. And here's coffee to go," I said as I handed him his coffee the way he liked it.

He nodded, taking the box from me. "Thank you, and remember what I told you."

I could feel Linda's gaze following us as I escorted the Sheriff to the door. "Goodnight, Willard."

"Take care, Penny."

The moment I turned the lock on the door Linda let out a massive exhale of air. "That was so intense."

"Yeah, thanks a lot for trying to run out on me," I quipped.

"No point in both of us going to jail," Linda shrugged.

"Gee, thanks. Real solidarity sister."

"I can't believe how desperate he is for our help," Linda continued.

I laughed, returning myself behind the counter to continue the prep work for the morning. "Only you would get that out of that conversation. He was telling us that we better watch our step."

"No," Linda insisted, as she leaned in, getting her face close to mine. "What he was doing was telling us who the next person we should interrogate is. Would someone do that unless they wanted our help?"

"Are you crazy? He did no such thing."

Linda frowned flopping back onto her stool. "You disappoint me, Penny Preston. I would have thought by now some of these detective skills would have started rubbing off. I guess you're just a slow learner."

"Please, do enlighten me," I snarled, filling the next batch of pre-greased muffin tins with batter.

"The sister?" she exclaimed. "The Sheriff wants us to question the sister. Why else reveal to us that she hated her brother? I mean, of course, the Sheriff had no idea we were already getting there ourselves from what we found out after talking with Brik."

I opened my mouth but had no answer to her statement. It was an odd thing to share. "And just what do we say to this sister?"

Linda looked off into nothing, biting her bottom lip. "You leave that to me, I've got a plan."

"That's what I'm afraid of," I muttered.

∾

CHAPTER TEN

I BENT OVER, retrieving the last box of blueberry muffins I had under the counter. Every day I made more delicious treats, and every day more customers showed up. Everyone wanted to catch a glance of the coffeehouse killer. Well, that's what the gossip columnist in the city had dubbed me in their opinion pieces. I wondered if they saw me in person they would still think of me as a murderer. I placed the box on the counter and rang up the young, handsome gentleman who tried to act like he wasn't filming me on his iPhone, even though I was quite confident he was.

To my left, I could feel someone's eyes boring into the side of my skull as I worked. I tried to avoid turning and looking, assuming it was just another curious stranger, but I couldn't take it any longer.

"Linda! When did you get here?" I gasped as I turned and ran right into Linda while handing the young man his change.

"About six hipsters ago," she didn't lower her voice as she said this. She didn't care if she offended anyone. It was one of the things I liked about her—that she said what she thought. I often wished I had that sort of courage.

I smiled sweetly at the customer, as he turned to exit. I couldn't help but giggle as the door closed behind him because he was, in fact, quite clearly a hipster.

"If you want something to eat I would hurry and decide, I only have what's left in the case," I suggested to Linda.

"Does that mean if you sell out you can close early?" Linda inquired, her gaze fixed eagerly on me.

I shook my head, narrowing my eyes at her. "I mean if I sell out I still have coffee to sell."

"Nobody wants just coffee," Linda grumbled.

"Expresso," the man in thick black rimmed glasses, that stood in front of me ordered.

"What does this look like, a Starbucks?" Linda hissed, as she rolled her eyes.

"I'm so sorry, please excuse my friend," I offered, before flashing an annoyed glare in Linda's direction. "I'm afraid she doesn't get a lot of human contact at the asylum."

Linda had chuffed before she muttered under her breath, "not likely."

"I'm afraid we're just a small town coffee shop with regular and decaf. But we do have delicious items in the case if you're interested."

The man crinkled his nose up in distaste, making him look like a pug for a moment. "Anything gluten free?" he asked, his tone clearly dissatisfied with my answer.

I smiled at his question; my cousin Brayden has celiac disease which inspired me to keep at least one gluten-free item on the menu. "I do," I stated as if I were a peacock placing my plumes proudly on display. "My famous easy-peasy peanut butter cookies only have three ingredients. Peanut Butter, sugar, and egg. Would you like one?"

He frowned and sighed. "I'm allergic to peanuts." Without another word, he turned and walked out of the shop.

"Oh, please, come again," Linda yelled after him before turning to me, and under her breath, she whisper-shouted, "or even better, never again."

"Linda, stop," I scolded her, even though I completely agreed.

"These people are insufferable; I don't know how you manage."

"Welcome to Half Day Coffeehouse. Can I help you?" I asked, looking over the counter at a very young and attractive couple who just came through the door. I wondered if they were married. I imagined them wearing matching sweaters at Christmas as they walked their matching Bichons.

"Do you think that's her?" The petite blonde woman stage whispered into the man's ear next to her. I considered letting her know that her whispering skills left much to be desired, but then decided that it would take far too much effort to engage in a witty exchange. I was still exhausted from a late night of baking and an early morning of sick dogs. One of the more recent rescue dogs I'd taken in seemed to be suffering from some stomach ailment. I was quite relieved I had remembered to keep him quarantined from the other dogs after he arrived.

The man cleared his throat. "Yes, hello. We will take three dozen blueberry muffins."

"Three dozen," I gasped.

"Yes, we're picking them up for our office," the blonde interjected with a smile that looked genuine, but I was certain it was not.

"I'm afraid what I have in the case is all I have left of everything," I answered.

The two conversed for a moment before they both looked up at me and with a smile the man stated, "We'll take everything in the case."

My mouth fell open. There had to be at least fifty various

pastries left in the case. "Everything?" I repeated as I glanced at Linda and then back at the customers.

"Yes, we'll just let them pick and choose what they want. That's so much easier," the woman replied.

Linda jumped to her feet. "I'll help! You ring them up." She darted around the counter and popped open the largest box I carried, then started to load the items in one by one.

"Are you okay?" I asked, my eyebrows drawn together.

"Of course, but after this don't you think it's wise to close. I mean no more pastries and the customers will be irritated," Linda suggested. I checked out the young couple, not replying to Linda. Something was up with her, and I couldn't ask her in front of customers.

With the stack of boxes secured in their arms, the couple smiled, gave me one last lingering stare and then exited. I grinned as I saw the next person in line was Neilson Woodberry, the sweet elderly song leader from the Presbyterian church down the street. "Hello Mr. Woodberry, can I have just one moment?"

He nodded as he stared at the empty pastry case, a look of disappointment lingering in his eyes. I turned and pulled Linda toward the back of the counter area.

"Spill it," I whispered. "Why do you want me to close early?"

"Okay, don't be angry."

"Anytime you start off like that I am most certainly going to be mad. What did you do?"

"So you know Jack's sister, Jill Egerton?"

"Yesss?" I drew out my response as I emphasized my irritation.

"Well, she's a bridesmaid in Wendy Wellington's wedding. I happen to be the one working on those dresses."

"And?" I pressed.

"And I called her and told her that I lost her measurements and needed her to come in for another fitting."

"You what?" I shouted, my heart pounded as I felt my blood pressure rise.

"Oh, come on. It's the perfect cover to ask her some questions about her brother," Linda argued.

"Of course it is. I mean, I can just see it now. Let's see what the inches on your bust is... Did your brother like busts or was he a leg man? Any reason someone would want to kill him?" I snarled, closing my eyes, trying to calm myself.

"Penny?" Linda whispered quietly.

"Yes?" I murmured, unable to look at her.

"I think she can help us. I just ... have a feeling."

"Is that right?" I grumbled. "When will she be here?"

Linda glanced up at the clock on the wall. "Twenty minutes. It was the only time she had available."

I turned toward the waiting line and walked back to the register. "If I can have everyone's attention." I waited for the line to quiet. "I'm afraid that last couple bought me out of my baked goods. I do have some coffee left which I can offer on the house."

Linda sprang into action, setting out the to-go cups on the counter. I filled them one after another as the crowd ascended, taking a cup and offering their thanks. Once all the patrons had retrieved their complimentary cup of coffee and exited the coffeehouse, I locked the door, flipped the sign to closed, and pulled off my apron, tossing it across the counter.

"Come on, Piper. You can assist Mommy with an interrogation," I called after my curvy Dachshund companion. She followed me to the door that led through the dog shelter and went out the back stairs up to Linda's sewing studio.

"Oh, you're not going to regret this. I think she could blow this case wide open." Linda insisted. I said nothing. There was nothing to say. I had to figure out who killed Jack

Egerton before the last person they could point their finger at would be me.

I picked Piper up as she had a tough time with stairs due to her short legs, and exited out the back. The door thunked closed behind me, and I had that sinking feeling in my stomach like I was getting ready to make one of the biggest mistakes of my life. I had that same feeling the day I married my ex-husband, and on the day I had the car accident that created the link between Piper and myself. I hoped this time my instinct was wrong.

∼

CHAPTER ELEVEN

IF I HADN'T KNOWN Linda for years and seen the clothing she made with her own two hands, I would never have believed she was a seamstress. Don't get me wrong, she was an artist with a needle and thread, but I had never seen someone as skilled as she was when she was in detective mode. She'd most certainly missed her calling.

"What are you going to say?" I asked, sitting in the high back chair near the electric fireplace on the wall.

"I thought I'd start with, did you kill your brother?"

"Linda!" I exclaimed, pulling Piper in closer to my body. "You can't." At that moment, there was a knock on the door, and we both gasped.

"Don't be ridiculous," she hissed. "Of course I'm not going to say that."

"What are you going to say?" I pressed, my heart now racing.

She paused, her hand hovering over the doorknob, "I guess I'll figure that out as I go."

Linda opened the door and smiled at Jill Egerton. Jill was

an everyday woman. She wore no makeup that I could tell, and her hair was pin straight, and she dressed neatly.

"Jill, hello, I'm so glad you could make it in," Linda said in a bubbly voice I had never heard uttered from her lips. It made me uneasy.

"I didn't have much choice, did I?" Jill answered back, tight-lipped.

"No, I suppose you didn't," Linda forced through gritted teeth. "Please, come in."

Jill Egerton's eyes immediately fixed on me as soon as she stepped inside.

Linda closed the door behind her and began the introductions. "Jill I'm not sure if you've ever met my landlord, this is—"

"I know exactly who she is," Jill interjected, her head snapping back in Linda's direction. My stomach began to do flips, and I had to fight the urge to run out of the door through which she had just arrived. "What is she doing here?"

"Oh, umm, well ..." Linda fumbled with her words, a reasonable explanation for my presence escaping her.

"Does this have to do with all the questions you two have been asking around town about my brother?" Jill demanded, shifting her glare between the two of us. This wasn't going as smoothly as we had anticipated.

Just then an image of Piper's favorite hiding space under my bed popped into my mind. My little Dachshund was trying to tell me she wanted to be anywhere but here right now. "I know," I whispered in her floppy copper colored ear. "Me too."

"What was that?" Jill practically shouted, and the soft-spoken vision I once had of Jill Egerton faded away. Could she have murdered her brother? Did she have the rage it took?

"I'm sorry, I was just talking to my dog," I offered.

"I bet you were!" she snapped.

"Please Jill, we didn't mean to upset you," Linda pleaded, raising her hands into the air. She took a step toward Jill causing Jill to stumble further into the room.

"Did you even lose my measurements?" she snapped. She was smart, I had to give her that. Linda didn't say a single thing in response, her mouth falling open. Jill struggled for a moment to find what to say herself. "I can't believe you would do something so cruel," she said, her voice trembling.

"Cruel?" Linda asked.

"Jill, we weren't trying to be cruel," I added, pushing myself deeper into the chair. Piper tucked her long snout between the arm of the chair and my body.

"Don't you speak to me!" she shrieked, a fiery look in her eyes. I pursed my lips and shook my head. *This isn't happening,* I told myself.

"Penny didn't do anything," Linda defended me. I wished she wouldn't. I felt like I had done something. I invaded this poor woman's privacy while she was grieving for her brother.

"That's for the law to decide," she threw back at Linda matter-of-factly, an indignant look on her face.

Linda lifted her chin defiantly and laughed. "You can't possibly be dumb enough to think Penny was the one who killed your brother."

I shrank into myself even more than I already was, relieved Linda's statement had shifted Jill's angry eyes in her direction. "Don't you ever call me dumb. People did see them arguing at her coffee shop; it would be a reasonable conclusion that she's now trying to cover her tracks."

I cringed and my nose scrunched up into my face for a moment. It wasn't just wild speculation in my mind anymore. People around Wyoming did, in fact, view me as someone who could have murdered Jack Egerton.

"Penny Preston no more killed your brother than I am a size six," Linda fired back.

"So you say," Jill muttered.

"So common sense says, and I suspect you're too smart to know so. If Penny was the murderer then why would she be risking her neck going around town and asking questions to try and find the real killer."

"Like I said, maybe she's just trying to throw off suspicion," Jill argued.

"Jill," I began in a soft voice, my heart pounding in my chest. "I know you don't know me, and you have no reason to believe me, but I didn't kill anyone. I won't lie. I did argue with your brother about a missing dog he was supposed to bring me that never showed up. But that was it. I wish I knew why he was in the shelter that night."

Jill squirmed as she listened to me, clearly fighting the urge to strangle me, or worse.

"Please, just listen one more second and then you can call the police if you want. I'm not going to tell you I am trying to find the killer because it's what your brother deserves, and it's not even because I want to make sure they don't suspect me —though that isn't a bad motivating factor. I'm trying to find out who killed your brother because I go home every night scared that whoever did it, is coming back for me."

There it was, the most vulnerable and real answer I could give her.

Jill's shoulders slumped as she crossed the room and plopped down onto a small loveseat, sinking back into it. She shrugged and said, "I know you didn't kill him," and then she sighed.

"You do?" I gasped.

"You do?" Linda repeated sounding even more surprised.

"Of course I do. You dedicate your free time to finding

cute little puppies homes, and you look like you probably get winded climbing a set of stairs," Jill grumbled.

"Uh, thanks? I think?" I grimaced, suddenly feeling much more self-conscious about my fitness level. I mean I know I'm a little curvy, but winded from stairs?

"Plenty of people wanted my brother dead, but I doubt you were at the top of that list," Jill continued. "I just thought Jack was paranoid."

"Paranoid?" Linda asked, moving to sit next to Jill, her big blue eyes wide open.

Jill sighed, "Yeah, he told me people were after him."

"Who?" Linda pressed.

"Everyone. You name it. Jack thought everyone was spying on him. It wasn't until he stole the jewels our mother left us that I realized he wasn't crazy." Jill bent forward, placing her head in her hands for a moment, then continued. "When I saw they had gone missing I knew Jack was the only person that had access. He was avoiding me, so when I started asking around about him, I realized how many other people he had hurt. My brother was a good for nothing con artist."

"He was your brother," I reminded her.

"He was a crook. No wonder he was paranoid about people being out to get him, he swindled everyone he encountered. Am I glad he's dead? Of course not. Am I surprised? Not in the slightest," Jill hammered home just how disgusted she was by her late brother.

"It sounds like you didn't have much of a soft spot for him," Linda interjected. I shot a disapproving glance her direction, but she was too engrossed in Jill Egerton's tale to notice me.

"I loved him, sure, but I also hated him. In the end, he named me as beneficiary on his life insurance. That money will help pay for his funeral," Jill said.

As soon as she said the words a chill went down my spine. If she loved him, I couldn't fathom how she could be speaking of a life insurance policy.

Her head jerked back and forth between myself and Linda. "And if either of you think I could have killed him for the life insurance, think again. After funeral expenses, I will be lucky to buy myself a lunch."

I gave Linda a sharp look. Her behavior for a grieving sister seemed odd, to say the least. Did Linda feel the same as I did? If she did, she wasn't letting on.

"Nobody thinks you killed your brother," Linda assured her. I considered chiming in that I wasn't too sure about that statement but then thought better of it. "Is there anyone who sticks out who may have been lurking around lately? Someone out of the ordinary?"

Just as Linda spoke, Piper sent me the image again of the person in the red scarf she had seen on the night of the murder.

"Not that I can think of," Jill replied.

"Do you own a red scarf?" I inquired.

"What?" The question caught in Jill's throat for a second. "Why does that matter?"

I shrugged, trying to sound nonchalant. "Just curious."

"No, I don't."

"Have you noticed anyone in a red scarf?" I asked. I could feel Linda's stare fixed on me.

Her brows stitched together as she considered the question. "Why? Does it have to do with who killed Jack? Do you ladies know something?"

I shook my head, disappointed. "It's probably nothing, just covering our bases."

"I suppose Tommy Bishop wears a red scarf, I mean, at least I think he does," she offered. "He's been Jack's best friend since grade school. Does he know something about who killed my brother?"

"No, I'm sure he doesn't. Just a silly question," I replied.

Jill made an ugly face and pulled herself up off the couch and crossed the room to the door of Linda's apartment. "Yes, I think I've had enough of amateur detective play time for one day." She lingered at the open door, looking over her shoulder. "I hope you find who did this to Jack, even if he did deserve it."

"We will don't worry," Linda assured her, standing and moving close to her. She reached a hand out to place on Jill's shoulder, but Jill was already out the door.

As soon as Jill left and the door closed, I exclaimed, "How can you promise her that? We have no idea how to find the killer. She could be the killer for all we know."

Linda looked as though she was lost in thought. "Jill isn't the killer."

"And what tells you that? All your years of keen detective work on the police force? Oh, yeah. That's right, you're a seamstress who just likes reading about crimes," I barked in response.

She was quiet, staring at her shoes. I waited another moment for her to respond, but she didn't. She didn't move. I stood, Piper under my arm and moved closer. I swallowed hard, sucked in a sharp breath and apologized, "I didn't mean to hurt your feelings. That was mean of me to say."

Linda's head snapped up, and her eyes were wide, and she wore a smile from ear to ear. "I know that Jill Egerton did not kill her brother the same way I knew how to get you to feel bad for the way you just spoke to me. I know people and Jill is not a killer."

"You're not right in the head Linda Louise," I scoffed.

"I can't argue with that statement. But now I have some alterations to get to so you should skedaddle."

"The bridesmaid dresses?"

"Nope," Linda shook her head. "Patricia Dooley's latest diet craze alterations. I swear letting her clothes in and out is like a game of whack a mole—just when I think I'm done, she's back again."

"Linda, you're terrible," I said as I walked to the door.

"I didn't say it was bad that she's a bigger girl. I mean, hey, I'm not exactly Twiggy over here," she joked. Being a shorter woman the extra thirty pounds she carried was visible, but did nothing to detract from her cuteness. "I'm just saying it can't be good to go up and down like that. Look what happens to a rubber band after it's been stretched back and forth too much."

"Goodbye Linda," I chirped, exiting through the doorway as she closed the door behind me. I headed to the coffee shop and decided I would walk the dogs and then get to baking. I was determined, tomorrow would be the day I made enough delicious treats for the crowd.

～

CHAPTER TWELVE

SOMEHOW MY PHONE manages to ring most often when I'm elbow deep in batter, or eight leashes are wrapped around my wrists. Tonight, it had managed to ring at least four times while I was indisposed. As I pulled the last batch of blueberry muffins out of the oven and placed my easy-peasy peanut butter cookies in the display case, I glanced at the screen of my phone, expecting to see that the fourth missed call had been from Linda. I was only down a flight of stairs from her, but if she didn't feel like making the trip out of her cozy studio, nothing would move her. Much to my surprise, the last call I missed was in fact not Linda, but Deputy Handsome. He will always be branded with that nickname in my thoughts.

An image of Deputy Handsome popped into my mind. He was scratching Piper's belly in it. I glanced down at my porky friend who stared back up at me with wide longing eyes. I smiled, "I like him too." I confessed.

I decided I would call him back after we were home. I was so frustrated after selling out of baked goods every single day since poor Jack's murder, that I was determined not to underestimate another day. Since leaving Linda's studio after our inappropriate grilling of Jill Egerton, I had been either baking or on doggie duty. The shop was now stocked with more confectionary goodies than I carried on even the busiest of holidays.

"Ready to go home girl?" I asked, bending down to slip Piper's leash on. She smiled back at me. Now some people would probably consider me crazy for saying this, but I am certain that my Dachshund smiles. Am I certain that they all do this? Of course not, but I also doubt that many dogs have a psychic connection with their owners.

"Bacon? Again?" I laughed at the image in my head. She continued with her smile.

I moved to the door that led to the animal shelter area. I know there was a lot of town chatter around town when I decided to put an animal refuge in the space that was connected to the rear of the coffeehouse. Even more chatter that I must be nuts when I connected the space to the coffee-house with a door, but I had a vision. And it came true when the first little girl and her parents made their way into the shelter as they waited for the line to die down. An adoption was made that day, a family created, and I knew I did the right thing by using our foot traffic to help these dogs find homes.

My heart sank, the problem was now all I could think when I reached for the door handle wasn't that first family, but instead about what happened in that small room to Jack Egerton. A life that was suddenly over. Why? It didn't make sense.

Jill had made it clear when we spoke to her that there was no love lost between her and her brother, but was Linda right? Was there no way that a little bad blood between siblings could lead to murder, or was Linda just unwilling to admit someone as harmless looking as Jill appeared to be could be a stone-cold killer? If she admitted that, perhaps she would also have to admit to herself that I was capable of such an act.

I stopped myself, reminding my wild imagination that I was being ridiculous. And besides, the police were investigating everyone who might be a suspect, based on what the Sheriff said, Jill wasn't being overlooked.

It seemed the more people we spoke to in Wyoming, the longer our suspect list grew. I needed to go home and jot down everything Linda and I had observed and get it to Deputy—just as I turned the doorknob and pushed open the door I remembered the missed call from Deputy Handsome. I would write everything down we had learned and then call him.

Immediately when I made my way through the door, Piper began to bark, causing the others to break out in a violent ruckus as well. "What are you all—" My breath caught in my throat as if it were a boulder. Tommy Bishop stared in through the small square window that led to the rear parking lot.

I scooped Piper up in my arms, trying my best to subdue her. "It's alright girl," I whispered. Then the debate in my head started. Should I open the door? No one would blame me if I didn't, after all, a woman alone at night. He was shouting something, not in an angry tone, but a more inconvenienced one, from the other side of the glass square. Maybe I should run. I couldn't get by him, and if I did, where would I go? Would I race him back to my house? I considered for a second pulling out my phone and dialing Derrick up, but he had already warned me to stay away from this case, what would he think I'd been up to?

The decision was made, with Piper under my arm I took a step forward and opened the door that led to the parking lot. The dogs all began to stir again as he moved into the space with me. I stumbled back, closing the gap between myself and the door that led into the coffeehouse.

"It's freezing out there," I noted, noticing he was not wearing a red scarf. I wondered, was it because he didn't have one or maybe a much more sinister reason, like his red scarf was covered with Jack Egerton's blood.

Tommy blew hot breath on his hands after pulling the exit door closed behind him.

"I'm afraid we're not doing any more adoptions tonight, but if you come back in the morning, we can discuss it," I rambled on nervously.

"Do you know who I am?" he asked. He had been in the coffee shop countless times on his way to work. He was always polite and never skimped on the tip jar.

"Of course, you're Tommy Bishop."

"I see, so you do know. Do you also know Jill Egerton?" he continued, and I thought I might have to pick my stomach up off the floor.

"We've met," I downplayed the recent interaction.

"Yeah, I heard that when I ran into her tonight."

"Is that right?" I feigned ignorance.

"She was pretty upset, asking me if I knew anything about Jack's death," he answered.

"Yeah? I wonder why she would do that. I mean you don't, right?"

Tommy just looked at me for a second. At that moment, I wanted to ask him a thousand questions, and I also wished he would never say another word to me. It was quite a confusing bundle of emotions I was having heaved on myself.

"You weren't at the funeral, yesterday," he noted as he watched me.

I swallowed hard, "You mean Jack's?"

He nodded.

"Yeah, I know, I didn't think it was appropriate for me to

be there." Tommy looked confused by my answer. He worked as an engineer at a 3D printing company, and every time I had seen him before he had never appeared so unkempt. His hair appeared as if it hadn't been brushed by more than his fingers in days. A week's worth of facial hair climbed its way across his chin and cheeks—and this wasn't the super attractive kind of beard, it was spotty and completely worn down to the bare skin in areas.

"I can imagine," he started, not taking his eyes off of me. "It must be hard with everyone thinking you're a murderer."

"I doubt everyone thinks I'm a murderer."

"Oh, no. I believe they do."

"Well, I'm not," I assured him.

"How come you don't serve those fancy coffee drinks with designs in them?" he asked, shifting his gaze around the room at the dogs. They were no longer barking at him, but they were wheezing and whimpering to make sure their presence wasn't forgotten.

"Excuse me?"

"Jack always said how he wished you guys would make those special drinks; you know the ones with hearts in the foam and stuff."

"I see, I guess you and Jack must have been close," he didn't respond. "My Aunt was the one that established the coffeehouse, and she never saw much reason for anything besides a strong cup of coffee. After she passed away, it never crossed my mind to change things from the way she'd done them for so many years."

I waited for him to say something, but his eyes were still darting around the room. "Tommy, can I get you something? A Buckeye perhaps? On the house." "What?" He shook his head as if he were clearing away the cobwebs. "No, I don't want a Buckeye!"

I was almost afraid to ask but knew I had to. "Then what do you want?"

"I wanted to see where—where it happened."

Tommy was not the killer. I was nearly certain—as certain as Linda was of Jill's innocence and I couldn't explain it either. He was disturbed by what happened to his friend, although I did sense he knew something more about what happened to Jack. I wondered if Linda would agree with my deduction skills.

"You miss him," I stated, my eyes fixed on his fists that were balled up at his side.

My forehead wrinkled as my eyebrows shot up in realization. Of course he missed him; they were best friends. He wouldn't be here wanting to see exactly where he died unless he wasn't plagued by the loss of Jack. This had to be proof that Jack wasn't all bad. At least one person seemed to care that he was gone.

"I like your coffee," he muttered, and I was certain I had misheard him.

"I'm sorry, what did you say?"

He shook his head, as though he wasn't quite sure what he was talking about himself. "I said that Jack wanted you to make specialty cups of coffee, but I thought you should know, I've been drinking your coffee since you moved in with your Aunt and I don't believe that you've ever made a bad cup."

I smiled. "Thank you. If you wanna know a secret, I scorched my very first pot I brewed here. My Aunt had to show me the special trick to get the burners not to overheat."

"I liked your Aunt too," he added. I could see he was uncomfortable talking about Jack. I needed to know what he knew, and the best way would be getting him to come inside and talk to me.

"She was a very special lady." I turned sideways and motioned toward the door that led back into the coffeehouse.

"How about I brew us a pot, and we can talk about all the great memories we have. Me of my Aunt, and you of Jack?"

I took a deep breath as I watched him mull over his decision regarding my invitation. I swallowed hard and opened my mouth to turn up the pressure. He didn't give me a chance.

His eyebrows raised and he looked at me as though I had just spontaneously sprouted a third eye on my forehead. "I have to go," he exclaimed.

He turned to walk away, and panic setting into my gut. My opportunity to find out what exactly Tommy knew was slipping away. "Um, well, are you sure?" I hesitated before continuing. "You know, if you want to talk, it might help."

"Why would I want to talk to the prime suspect in my friend's murder?" he flashed me an icy glare, but it quickly melted away.

"I think you know I didn't kill Jack," I continued, exhaling a deep breath after the words left my lips. It felt right to say them, to openly defend myself. Day after day countless people filtered into the coffeehouse, their accusing eyes fixed on me, and I could say nothing. It wouldn't have mattered if I did. It was more interesting gossip for everyone to assume I was guilty of such a terrible crime.

"What's that supposed to mean?" Tommy snapped defensively. "I don't know who killed him. I also don't know you."

"No, I suppose you don't."

"It very well could have been you," he snapped.

"I could say the same thing about you," I replied.

I laughed, though his expression revealed he was more shocked by my statement. "Why would you say that?" he demanded, his voice cracking. He didn't wait for me to answer. "What would make you say something like that?" he repeated.

I shook my head. "I only meant that we don't know who

killed your friend, but it obviously wasn't either of us who did it. I doubt you would have come here if you really thought I was the one who killed your friend."

Tommy scoffed. "Maybe. Or maybe I don't scare easily."

"Really? Because you seem a little shaken?"

His head jerked around wildly, his eyes darting from side to side. "I don't know what you're talking about."

"Is someone bothering you?" I asked pointedly.

He shook his head again as his eyes widened. "You don't know what you're talking about." He paused and looked over his shoulder anxiously, looking out the window that led to the parking lot. His head snapped back in my direction. "And if you know what's good for you, you'll stop poking your nose around Jack's death."

"You said it yourself; I'm the police's prime suspect. If I don't help them catch Jack's killer, I could be looking at being fingered for a crime I didn't commit."

He looked me up and down. "No jury would every think you could have done this. Please, I'm telling you to let the police handle this."

"You do know something," I state boldly. "You have to tell me."

Tommy bolted for the door, only hesitating a moment. "Don't say I didn't warn you." His breath caught in his throat when he turned to exit, Linda was standing directly in his path.

"Why Tommy Bishop," Linda started, her voice laced with suspicion. "What brings you out here this late?"

I nodded in her direction, giving a half smile to let her know I was all right. Tommy huffed, before pushing past Linda and making his way down the street. Linda scurried up the steps, pulling the door closed and locking it behind her. She peeked out the small window for good measure, just to ensure Tommy hadn't indeed decided to turn around and finish the conversation.

Her head immediately snapped in my direction. "Are my ears deceiving me or did I just hear Tommy Bishop threaten you?"

I shook my head. "More like warned me."

"Not sure I see a difference but what exactly was he warning you about?"

"If I had to guess, he knows who the killer is, and he knows they don't like us snooping around," I answered.

"Is he working with them?"

I pulled Piper close to me and gave her a hug, rubbing my chin against her smooth back, reassuring her that we were okay. "I don't think so. I think he's scared too."

"What exactly did he say?" Linda pressed.

"Just that I should let the police handle Jack's case," I answered, thinking about the statement briefly. "Maybe we should."

"Maybe we should what?"

"Let the police handle this," I replied, pressing my back against the door that led to the shop with a sigh. "I think we should call the Sheriff and let him know about Tommy's little visit."

"Oh yeah?" Linda quipped. "And tell them that Tommy told you to let the police handle things? They will give him a stinking medal."

"Tommy isn't going to tell us anything so what do you suggest we do?" I asked, out of ideas.

Linda lifted a finger to her chin, tapping it repeatedly, deep in thought. Had she had a deerstalker cap and a pipe I could have mistaken her for Sherlock Holmes himself. "We wait, and we watch."

"What?"

"If Tommy Bishop knows something he'll slip up sooner or later," she declared.

"And if he turns up dead, too? That will be on us."

"I guess we'll just have to keep a really close eye on him."

"I don't have a good feeling about this," I confess.

"I wouldn't expect anything else from you," Linda laughed. "Now come on, I'll give you and Piper a ride home."

CHAPTER THIRTEEN

THE MORNING WAS STILL and the air cold as I stepped out of bed and placed my feet on the icy hardwood floors. I always kept a pair of slippers next to my bed, but they had been in the bathroom the night before—the dark and when you're all by yourself, scary, bathroom. I decided just to run and jump into bed, pull the blankets over my head and hope my imagination didn't kill me before morning. Luckily, I had awakened. No killer, lurking through the night had murdered me in my sleep; just Piper cuddled up next to my head.

It ended up the darkness of the early morning hours didn't help make my home feel any warmer or safer. Since Tommy Bishop's visit last night, all I could think about were that shadows all around me, hiding the faceless men who were hunting me.

A clear image formed in my mind of the coffeehouse and the other dogs in the kennel. I glanced over at Piper who was now staring at me, wide awake.

"Good thinking," I smiled. "Safety in numbers."

I wasted no time getting ready, and rushing out of my house and in the direction of the shop, Piper was sporting her favorite winter parka that Linda had sewn for her last year. It was early, and not many people were usually out at this time, but I was surprised to see no-one stirring. With the recent excitement, especially, there was usually a stray car or two driving around.

When I approached the coffeehouse, I considered slipping in the back, even though I knew it would wake the foster dogs before I was ready to get them out for their morning walk. Much to my surprise, as I approached, I could see there was no line. In fact, there wasn't a single living soul waiting outside the coffeehouse. I paused anxiously but then decided I was here earlier than usual, and that must be the explanation.

I entered through the front, placed all the pre-made batters into the oven so the treats that were better served hot and fresh would be ready just in time for opening. Then I started on the kennel chores. It was nice to have so much to do to distract myself from my overactive imagination.

The dogs were walked, fed, and settled in with full bellies for their early morning nap by the time I got the coffee brewing. At this point, I could see a couple of people milling about outside the front door. My phone buzzed—it was Linda. She needed to talk. She had a theory that was forming and it was better not to discuss it over the phone.

"If you say so," I said as I rolled my eyes. Knowing Linda, it was some crazy off the wall theory.

"I'll meet you at the coffee shop at closing," Linda added, hanging up before I could respond. I smiled, no matter what harebrained idea she had come up with I at least knew it would be entertaining.

My first customer of the morning was no surprise. Mrs. Collins worked at one of the large banks in the city. For years, she would come in before work for a coffee to go, nothing else. She was on what she explained was a keto diet. Basically, it meant carbs were the devil. It immediately sounded like a diet I could never succeed at so I usually quit listening around that time. She liked my shop because her unique request to put butter in her coffee was not a problem. I hadn't seen her since the— well, since all the craziness began. I hoped she wasn't buying into the coffeehouse killer theories about me.

"Ugh," she sighed. "I am so glad all those crowds died off. I mean really sweetie, I love your coffee, but no way am I going to wait forty-five minutes for a cup."

I looked outside, my usual line wrapped around the block consisted of four people. "I'm so sorry you've been inconvenienced like that," I offered, my stomach sinking as I recalled the record-breaking number of pastries I spent the previous day making. "Large black with a pat of butter."

She tossed a five on the counter and instructed me to keep the change. Mrs. Collins never tipped. It felt strange, and I remembered to thank her after she was already out the door and headed to her overpriced luxury car.

The remaining customers trickled in, then a few more, but it felt much more normal than it had since the great Wyoming Coffee Killer drama began. I couldn't figure it out. Had people just suddenly lost interest? Hours went by with a slow, steady stream of customers. Part of me was relieved to have the target off my back, while the other part of me was dreading the idea of figuring out where I would find enough freezer space for the 200 muffins I had baked.

"Well, hello, Penny Preston," a cold voice came from behind me. I recognized it but assumed my mind had to be playing tricks on me.

I turned to see, in fact, I had been correct. Dara Mavin stood, staring back at me. She was impressively pulled together, thought given to her ensemble from the top of her head all the way down to her perfect peek-a-boo patent leather shoes. I wanted to ask her if her toes were cold in them, but decided that probably wouldn't be a splendid idea. Her eyes were no longer red and swollen, in fact, I would even go as far as to say she looked well rested. Why was she here? Had she come to tell me that she changed her mind and had decided to press charges on Linda and me for harassing her? I wouldn't blame her if she made that decision.

"Miss Mavin, hello," I offered respectfully, tucking a strand of my chestnut brown hair behind my ear. "What can I do for you today?"

"I have an order for the office," this was highly out of the ordinary as my friend Polly Hittle was normally the one who would come in with the order for the real estate firm.

"Oh, okay," I replied, reaching out and taking the small piece of paper from her delicate hand. I saw Polly's hand-writing on the note as I read the order of two dozen blueberry muffins. "What a relief," I smirked, attempting to fill the awkwardness with small talk.

"Excuse me?"

"I made hundreds of muffins expecting the same crowds I've had, but it has been relatively dead today," I explained.

"I'm so sorry to hear that you're no longer profiting off my dead boyfriend's death." My stomach sank at her words.

I was pretty sure I had just literally turned a shade of green, "I am so sorry. I didn't think before I said that. That must have sounded so insensitive of me."

"Geez, I'm kidding, calm down. You didn't hear?" she asked, leaning in as if she were nearly going to explode with her juicy piece of unknown gossip. The distressed grieving girlfriend I had met just days ago now seemed to have found a sudden peace with the death of her lover.

"Hear what?" I asked politely.

"A bunch of protesters climbed out onto the face of a building of one of the big corporations downtown and hung a banner that's exposing the company for breaking dozens of health codes or something," she shrugged, unsure of the specifics. "They're refusing to come down until their demands are heard. I guess it's being live streamed."

I was yesterday news. For now, the attention had shifted, and this brought me some small measure of relief.

"I hope they're okay," I add.

"As long as they don't detract from the open house I'm taking these muffins to. Polly has been planning the Mayweather mansion showing for over a month. She's so on edge."

I hadn't spoken to my friend in some time, distracted by my problems. "Tell her I said good luck," I said with a smile.

Dara lifted her eyebrows. "Yeah. Okay." Her response told me there was little chance my good wishes would ever make it back to Polly.

"Hey, Dara," I continued, placing the two large boxes full of muffins on the counter. "I meant to call you and apologize for my friend and me. That behavior was—"

"Completely uncivilized?" Dara interjected.

I offered a shameful nod, dropping my head.

"Yeah, it was." She said in a firm voice. A long silence followed before she added, "but I get it."

"You do?" I gasped, a little surprised by her statement.

"Don't get me wrong, what you did was completely insensitive, and I fully expect for you to come to me when you're finally ready to pull the trigger on buying a house," I felt sick again at the mention of yet another one of the many lies we seemed to be spreading around. "But I can relate to your predicament."

"Is everything okay?" I asked, a furrow crossing my brow.

Dara placed her dark gray Michael Kors purse on the counter and rummaged around inside of it for a moment before pulling a stack of papers free. She shoved them in my direction. "I thought you might like to look at these."

Looking down, I saw they were bank statements. "I don't understand."

"They're Jack's. There was some money missing from our joint account which I found deposited into his personal account. That wasn't all I found." She shook her head as her face turned multiple shades of red. I could see the break of trust had her furious.

"What do you mean?"

"Take a look for yourself. There are deposits all over that account from Happy Farms."

"Happy Farms?" I repeated, looking back down at the statements. "The meat packing plant?"

"Yes."

"Did he work there too?"

"Not that I knew of."

"Dara, I don't understand, if this seems out of the ordinary why wouldn't you take it to the police?" I inquired.

Her shoulders slumped, as she rolled her eyes. "Uh, because these also show that he was stealing money from me which I didn't mention to the Sheriff when he came to talk to me the first time and would clearly make me a suspect as well. I figured if anyone knew how that felt it would be you. Jack took enough from me. I'm not about to become a suspect in his murder."

"I see," I replied, thinking about her statement. "But what do you want me to do about it?"

"I don't know," she huffed. "Whatever detective thing you and that friend of yours do. Just figure this out."

"Dara, we're not detectives."

"You say you're sorry for the way you and your friend came after me and you want to make it up to me? Well, this is how."

I looked at her sympathetically. She looked strong, standing there in her perfectly fitted suit, but despite how hard she tried to hide it I could see the pain underneath the icy stare.

"I can't promise you anything," I added. "Do you mind if I hold onto these statements to show Linda?"

She nodded, paid, and grabbed the boxes of muffins. Over her shoulder, she called back, "I know you'll find the truth.

She left me standing there, wondering to myself if I would even know what the truth looked like when I finally saw it. I looked closer at the bank statements and the multiple circled deposits. I had to figure this out, for all our sakes.

≈

CHAPTER FOURTEEN

"Tell everyone they need to leave, close the doors and lock up," Linda ordered as she entered the coffeehouse.

"What? Why?" I moaned in confusion.

"I've cracked the case," Linda announced, with her arms raised above her head. "And we have work to do. Now everyone must go."

I looked around in an exaggerated manner. "Not sure if you noticed, but it's not exactly busy around here." I frowned, thinking again about the several hundred muffins I had baked in a very unfortunate miscalculation.

She repeatedly blinked, her head jerking back and forth, processing the scene. "Where's all the looky loos?"

"Apparently, I'm yesterday's news," I grimaced.

"What?"

I shrugged. "There was some sort of demonstration downtown today, and the police are having trouble bringing them in."

"Guns?" she gasped.

I shook my head. "Climbing gear."

"Okay, I'm not even going to pretend I understand what

you're talking about," Linda replied, approaching the empty counter and sitting on a stool across from me. "But none of that matters, I know who killed Jack Egerton."

My eyes widened. "You do?" I gasped.

"Okay, not the exact killer," she confessed. "But I have a theory that will narrow it down."

I nodded. "Theory, huh?"

"Last night, after Tommy's little visit, guess who I saw parked out in front of Jill Egerton's house?"

"What?" I exclaimed, my breath catching in my throat. "Did you call the police?"

"Why would I do that?" Linda scoffed, her brows stitching together. "I was the one who was inappropriately lurking."

"Well, that much we do agree on." I conceded. "But did it ever cross your mind that maybe I was wrong, and he is the killer, and he was going after Jill next?"

She paused, as she pondered my statement. "You know just when you were showing a sliver of possibility as a detective you go and toss out a silly statement like that."

"Linda, this isn't a game," I snapped, turning toward the telephone. "We should call the Sheriff. What if he hurt her?"

"Unless her kissing him is a cry for help, I think she's just fine," Linda was clearly proud of her revelation.

"Kissing?" I whispered, as the door chimed and in walked Violet, the local wedding cake baker.

I greeted her, and after serving her a cup of coffee and much to my relief, a muffin, I waited with a smile for her to exit. Once the door closed my neck snapped back like a rubber band toward Linda as I slammed my hands down on the counter causing the cash register to rattle.

"Kissing?" I repeated in disbelief.

She nodded, gleaming with pride as if she had just won the Olympic gold in spying.

While the news surprised me, I was having a little trouble connecting the dots to equal murder. "So you think it was Tommy?"

Linda tilted her head in thought. "Could be, or maybe Jill. Either way seems like we have a couple of conspirators on our hands."

"But why?" I questioned, as I shook my head. "It doesn't make sense. I can't work out what Tommy's motive would have been and Jill, I mean would she have killed her brother over money?"

Linda wrinkled her forehead and frowned a little. "I haven't worked out all the details, but people have killed for much less. Maybe Jack threatened Tommy and told him that if he didn't quit seeing his sister, he'd be sorry."

"But they were best friends, why would he do that? And seriously, if you're going to steal from your sister, do you think it would upset you if your buddy was dating her? He just doesn't strike me as the type who would have cared."

"I don't know, maybe Jill was so upset about her brother stealing from her she seduced her brother's best friend and convinced him to kill Jack," Linda continued.

"No, I don't buy that either. I don't know," I said, my words caused Linda to blush. "Did either of them honestly strike you as someone who would kill over something so ... petty."

"Don't be naive," Linda huffed. "I've wanted to kill you for much less."

I smirked at her. "Funny. But that's my point. I'm still here. To actually kill someone I just think there has to be more of a motive."

"Fine, do you have a better theory?"

I rocked back onto my heels. "Maybe," I answered, thinking of my visit from Dara. I had no idea why Jack's moonlighting at a second job would be something that would have gotten Jack killed, but it was all I had. What I couldn't shake was why would Jack have kept it a secret from Dara?

Linda nearly choked. "Let's hear it then."

"Dara Mavin came to see me earlier today," I continued, watching Linda's face morph into a shocked expression.

"Dara Mavin?" she blurted out. "As in Jack's Dara Mavin?"

I nodded, then waited to draw out the suspense. It wasn't very often I was ahead of Linda on information in this town, and it felt good to know something she didn't, even if it was just for a moment.

"Well?" she insisted, shaking her hands in the air.

The door chimed again, and I grinned. Two customers in a matter of minutes was more than I had had for the past two hours. I looked at the door, drinking in the perfect picture of Deputy Hanson. An image of him kissing me popped into my mind, and I glared down at Piper as I whispered, "Not funny."

"What's not funny?" he asked as he approached the counter.

"Huh?" I felt my face flush hot. "Oh nothing, what can I get for you today Deputy?"

He looked at Linda suspiciously who began to turn about five shades of red before his eyes. I could see not knowing why Dara came to see me was nearly killing her.

"Are you okay?" he asked, his eyes fixed on Linda.

"Of course. I'm okay, why wouldn't I be okay?" she exclaimed.

"Are you sure? You're bright red," he added.

"Thanks for pointing out my aging young man, it's called a hot flash! Would you like me to explain to you how that works for a woman my age?" she said sneering at him, and I couldn't help but snicker at her response.

"I-I didn't—" he stammered. "I'm sorry. I didn't mean to—"

"Just ignore her," I smiled at him. "Coffee?"

He nodded, relieved at my interjection. "For the Sheriff and me. Better give us a box of those muffins he loves so much too."

"Of course," I nodded and proceeded to pop open a cardboard box.

"Who are you dating these days Deputy?" Linda asked, flashing me a sideways smile.

He coughed, surprised by her question.

"You don't have to answer her," I suggested. "She's just trying to embarrass you. When you get to be her age not many things in life bring you joy, so you try to make everyone else around you just as miserable."

His speechlessness and dropped jaw expression melted into a soft smile. He glanced at Linda and then back at me. "It doesn't bother me at all. I'm not dating anyone if you must know."

His words created a flutter in my stomach.

"Oh, really?" Linda was practically salivating over the juicy information.

He shook his head. "No time. It wouldn't be fair to anyone I dated. I guess right now; I'm married to the job." The statement was cliche and one often used by those with commitment phobias; I made a puking motion when his back was turned, causing Linda to laugh. He turned back and gave me a puzzled glance.

As Linda spoke, he looked back at me, and I couldn't help blushing. I dropped my head, focusing on placing the last muffin safely inside and sealing the box. So much for my fantasies about Deputy Handsome.

"What if the right lady came along?" Linda pressed. I wanted to shake her.

I could feel his eyes still on my face as I made my way to

the register. "Well, I suppose," he hesitated. "If the right woman were to come along."

After I took his cash, I quickly handed him his change, slid the box of muffins and two coffees across the counter, offering my thanks. I turned back toward Linda and hoped he would take the hint and leave quickly. He did. I was weak around him, and I couldn't risk slipping up and saying something about Dara. She trusted me with that information and I was determined not to let her down.

"What was that all about?" I gasped staring at her wide-eyed.

"You were never going to ask him," Linda exhaled and shrugged her shoulders.

"Maybe because he's currently investigating a murder that I am a prime suspect in?"

"Speaking of prime suspect," Linda transitioned smoothly. "What did Dara Mavin have to say?"

"I shouldn't tell you after that stunt," I snarled. But we both knew I would. "Dara Mavin brought me these," I continued as I pulled out the bank statements and placed them on the counter in front of Linda.

She read over them, a puzzled look inching across her face. Eyebrows lifted she asked, "bank statements?"

"Not just any bank statements. These are for an account Dara knew nothing about. Apparently, they reveal that Jack had been moonlighting at the Happy Farms Plant."

"And?" she huffed, unimpressed.

"And he never told her about the job. Why keep that a secret from your lover?"

"It's shocking how creepy it is to hear you say the world lover," Linda groaned.

"Shut up," I commanded. "This is serious. What if he didn't tell her because he was hiding another girlfriend that worked there. Or, I don't know, something else."

Linda shrugged. "Maybe he wanted to treat her to a surprise gift."

"Did Jack Egerton seem like the romantic type to you?" I inquired with a doubtful stare.

She pondered quietly then asked, "When do you close?"

I glanced at my watch. "Fifteen minutes, why?"

"We're heading to Happy Farms," she announced.

"What? What happened to your theory about Tommy and Jill?" I asked, half teasing.

"Oh, please," she dismissive waved a hand in my direction. "You know as well as me that theory had more holes in it than a block of Swiss cheese."

I smiled.

"What are you grinning at?" she grumbled.

"Don't worry," I said, continuing to smile. "I won't make you say I'm a decent detective after all."

"No worries, I had no intention of saying any such thing," she added before walking to the exit and calling over her shoulder, "I'll meet you at the car in twenty."

My mind was swirling. I wasn't sure what our trip to Happy Farms would reveal. Would I finally find something that could help clear my name or would this trip lead to only more questions? "Just one viable clue would be nice," I moaned.

The image of the red scarf popped into my mind again. I bent down to rub Piper's belly, the red scarf, fixed in my thought. "Sorry girl, I guess we do have one solid clue, thanks to you. The killer was wearing a red scarf," I smiled as she looked up at me. "Maybe I should stick to baking, and you handle the detective work," I suggested before giving an apprehensive laugh.

~

CHAPTER FIFTEEN

As we drove through the large metal gate, parked, and stepped out of the car, my mind was swirling. I couldn't shake the notion that I should have told Deputy Hanson when I saw him, about the bank statements Dara gave me. Was this interfering with a police investigation? Had I crossed a line? Did the police already know about the moonlighting at Happy Farms as part of their investigation?

I fumbled through my purse and dug out the tiny spiral notebook with the pen shoved through the ring. After every person we spoke to I would pull out that notebook and jot down anything of importance in it. I'm not sure if it was because I thought it would help me solve the case or if because I wanted there to be some evidence in case one of the people I interviewed came back and killed me. As we walked, I flipped through the pages until I found a blank one and then placed it back in my purse, ready in case I had to jot something down quickly. From the corner of my eye, I could see Linda snickering.

"What?" I huffed.

"Oh nothing," she paused. "Sherlock."

I huffed. "Oh please, we know that title's reserved for you."

A smile peeled across her face from ear to ear as she pulled open the tinted glass door with the cartoon image of smiling farm animals printed on it. "You're right, let's call you Watson."

We approached the woman at the front desk. She didn't lift her head up as we came closer, her eyes fixed on her computer screen, and her fingers were furiously tapping away. She paused to push the glasses that were sliding down her nose back into place.

"Can I help you?" she asked, more sensing our presence than actually looking at us.

My heart began to race. I hadn't thought that far ahead. What could we say? We were there investigating a murder that occurred at my place of business. Maybe we could ask, did she know anyone around the company who seemed like the killer type? I bit my lip anxiously.

"Hi, yes, my niece asked me to come in and see if there were any checks that hadn't been picked up for her fiancé," Linda rolled into the lie like it was nothing. I watched in awe as she continued to weave her amusing story.

The woman at the desk finally stopped to look up at us, pulling off her ill-fitting glasses. "I'm sorry, who are you?"

"Oh, hi. I'm Linda, and Dara Mavin is my niece," she continued.

The woman smiled, pretending she knew what we were talking about, though the doubt in her eyes revealed we were only confusing her. "It's such a tragedy, what happened to her fiancé, isn't it?" We both waited, watching the secretary's expression. Nothing. "Why are you the one picking up the check?" she inquired.

"Oh, well, Dara had to show some clients who were in from out of town for just one day, some properties. She's an up and coming real estate star, you know?" Linda continued, the woman looked at me and then back at Linda. "Plus, I knew after Jack being murdered and all," she whispered these words, " coming here would be hard on her."

"Oh!" The woman gasped, suddenly realizing who exactly we were talking about. She looked around as if to make sure we were alone, leaned forward and whispered, "You know I didn't even know he had a fiancé. That makes it even more tragic."

I nodded, speaking at last, "It is, isn't it?" When the woman's eyes darted back at me, causing a strand of platinum blonde hair to come loose from her nearly perfect ponytail, I wished I had remained silent.

"And you are?" she inquired, her voice laden with suspicion.

"A friend," I replied, starting to fidget. "You know, just here for moral support."

"I see," the woman's response was slow, and I could see her processing my statement. Suddenly, as if a switch flipped inside her secretary brain, she shrugged her shoulders, gave us a professional smile and instructed us. "Mr. Egerton was a private contractor, so you'll have to speak with Oliver Flank. He would be the one to know if there were any outstanding unpaid hours. Take a seat, and I'll let him know you're here to see him." A second later her glasses were back on her face, and she was typing like the wind.

We thanked her, though I am confident she didn't hear us, and turned to take a seat in the barn themed waiting area. Everything around us gave the impression of a small-town farm. It was clever greenwashing, something I was familiar with from one of my many temp jobs back in San Diego. Greenwashing was an attempt by a company to make you think something that was likely heavily processed and very bad for you was, in fact, good for you.

I froze just before I took my seat. Linda didn't wait for me. She was already sitting and looking up at me. "What's wrong with you?" she asked, peering at my body, stuck in mid-air. Just above her head and to the right I saw a coat rack. There was a tan coat perched on it and hanging off that tan coat was a red scarf.

I spun toward the secretary and choked out the question, "Who does that coat belong to? The one with the red scarf?"

She paused, glancing up, irritated, and sighed before answering, "It's mine, why?"

"Oh—" I blurted, startled by her response. "I was just curious where you got that scarf."

"Excuse me?"

"I mean...uh, red, it's-uh-my favorite color," I stammered through my lie. In fact teal was my favorite color, it always had been since I first saw it in the ocean as a little girl.

"Happy Farms gives them out to all the employees. It's called barn red," she explained, though she clearly was not pleased she had to stop what she was working on to answer my question.

I forced an uncomfortable laugh. "I can't happen to buy one, can I?"

"Sorry, they were our incredible Christmas bonus this year. Employees only," she droned on, not waiting for me to walk away before continuing her work.

I rushed over to Linda's side, sitting in the chair next to her.

"What is wrong with you?" she grimaced.

"The killer works at Happy Farms," I whispered in her ear, my palms starting to sweat. "That is the same scarf that has been in Piper's visions to me."

"Are you certain?" she asked, jerking her head toward the red scarf hanging above her head.

"Don't look," I murmured, grabbing her arm tighter. "We have to get out of here."

"What? We're so close," Linda pleaded.

"We need to go tell the Sheriff what we know," I argued.

Linda rolled her eyes. "Yeah, I can hear it now. Willard, my dog, gave me a psychic vision that the killer was wearing a red scarf. You and I both know that would buy you a one-way ticket to crazy town lock up."

I raised my eyebrows, silent for a moment. "You might have a point," I admitted.

"Mr. Flank will see you now," the woman with the glasses called across the room, hanging up the phone. "Down that hall, through the double blue doors and then all the way at the end on the right."

Linda stood and said, "Great, thanks." She grabbed my arm and pulled me alongside her.

"I have a bad feeling about this," I hissed in her ear.

"Just stick with our cover story, and we'll be fine," she assured me.

≈

CHAPTER SIXTEEN

I YELPED as I went flying head first through the open door that led to the blue-walled room. My purse fell and slid across the floor; the notepad tucked inside tumbled out. I managed to catch myself with the heels of my hands before I planted myself cheek first onto the tile floor. Linda scurried past me, picking up my belongings.

"Are you okay?" I heard a faceless man's voice ask.

"Oh, don't mind her," Linda chimed. "She just got her legs yesterday." The next thing I felt was Linda gripping my bicep and pulling me upright to my feet.

"Yes, I-I'm so sorry. I'm a frightfully clumsy person," I added, brushing myself off and tucking my wild strands of hair behind my ears.

"Are you hurt?" the man asked, now standing and looking directly at me. My face flushed red, and I was unable to hide my embarrassment.

I forced a smile as I looked at the forty-something man with gray thinning hair and pale complexion. "Only my pride." I took a deep breath, stretched out a hand, and introduced myself. "I'm Penny Preston, nice to meet you." Linda grabbed my arm and squeezed as hard as she could. I wanted to cry out in pain, but at that moment I realized I had just broken cover and in fact given the man my real name.

I could see in his eyes he instantly recognized the name. "And I'm Linda Mavin," Linda interjected continuing with her story.

"Uh, yes," he replied, his eyes fixed on me. "And what exactly can I do for you ladies?" He waved a hand toward the chairs in front of his desk, and we took a seat. A warning sounded in my head as panic erupted inside of me at the idea that I had just shared my real name.

"Well, Mr. Flank," Linda continued. "It is Mr. Flank, isn't it?"

He nodded, a suspicious look on his face. I couldn't figure out if it was because he knew something or if it was because he thought a killer was sitting right in front of him. By now, even he had to have heard the news and my name tied to Jack's death. "Yes, Oliver Flank."

"Mr. Flank, my niece Dara Mavin was the fiancé of one of your recent employees," Linda replied. Oliver turned toward the window, standing and looking out through the blinds.

"Is that a fact?" His voice shook. He was nervous. "And you Ms. Preston, are you also related to Dara Mavin?"

"Oh, heavens no. Linda and I were just out to lunch together, and she asked if I minded if we stopped in here on the way back," I resisted smiling even though I was quite proud of my deception.

"Well I am so sorry to hear about Dara's loss, but I'm not really sure what I can do for you," he continued.

"Dara was curious if there were any checks Jack didn't pick up," Linda answered, as cool as a cucumber. "You know she's so overwhelmed with all the funeral expenses; another paycheck could go a long way."

"No," the man shook his head, not looking back at us, his

eyes fixed out the window. "He got everything that was coming to him.

"I bet he did," Linda muttered under her breath.

Oliver Flank whipped around. "What did you say?"

"Huh?" Linda gasped. "Oh me. Just that I'm sure he did get paid out."

"Sorry I can't help you more, but I do have a meeting to get to. Please relay to his fiancé how sorry I am for her loss." He turned and stood directly behind his chair.

"Do you mind me asking what Jack did for your company? I mean, he never even told Dara what his job was," Linda inquired, staying planted firmly in her seat.

"Yeah, of course. He was a ... um, dog catcher."

"Yes, we know that but we mean for you," I added.

"No, for us too. We're a meat packaging plant. We have a terrible problem with strays coming around."

"Is that a fact?" Linda asked with a grin. "I never realized that was a problem."

I stood, preparing for Linda and me to make our exit when I saw something out the window Mr. Flank had just been looking at that made my blood run cold. "Is that a Bernese Mountain Dog?" I exclaimed lifting a finger to point out the window, my mouth hanging open. That was the exact dog breed Jack and I had gotten into a heated argument about. It was the argument that had made me a suspect in his murder. There was a man in a brown uniform chasing the dog across the plant floor.

Mr. Flank side-stepped in front of the window, blocking my view, "Like I said, we get a lot of strays around here."

Just as he said these words, I saw a picture on the table behind his desk of him standing with an arm around Tommy Bishop. They were younger; perhaps it was in college.

"Yes, a stray, of course," I repeated, knowing full well there was no way someone had let a Bernese Mountain Dog wander off as just another stray. I returned his gaze, doing my best to keep it steady as I leaned forward and gripped Linda's forearm, pulling her upright. "We will pass the news along to Dara that there wasn't another check and be on our way."

"Thank you for your time, goodbye," Linda bellowed over her shoulder as I pulled her out the door. We didn't wait for him to reply. "What has gotten into you girl? You look like you've just seen a ghost."

"Worse," I answered, glancing back over our shoulder to ensure we weren't being followed. "I think I may have just seen a killer."

$\sim$

CHAPTER SEVENTEEN

WE HEADED BACK to the coffeehouse; the dogs would be dying for a walk by now. When we got there, we rushed straight inside, making no delay of discussing what we both had observed.

"You're certain that was the same Bernese Mountain Dog that Jack was supposed to bring to you?" Linda asked for at least the fourth time since I explained what I had seen.

"Of course I can't be certain since I never saw the dog, but how many Bernese Mountain Dogs do you see running around?" I quipped.

Linda shrugged, "I don't know, it's not like I'm a dog expert or something."

I opened the door that led to the kennel area and began leashing up the dogs to my left while Linda leashed the dogs on the right. "Sorry guys," I apologized. "You certainly haven't been getting enough play time have you?"

"You'd think they hadn't seen a human being in weeks by the way they're acting," Linda gave me a frustrated glance as she tried to wrangle the Labrador mix.

We walked quickly with the dogs down the rear steps,

closing the rear entrance to the kennel and headed down the alley, then left toward the park. The dog at Happy Farms kept flashing in my thoughts. It had just been for a brief second, as the dog darted out of my field of vision. I could have been mistaken. And was Tommy being friends with Oliver Flank any sort of smoking gun? Of course, they knew each other, that would make sense why Jack got the job in the first place. Tommy had referred him. But Tommy seemed scared of something. If Oliver were his friend, why be afraid.

"Did you happen to jot down in that notebook of yours what Mr. Flank's job title was?" Linda inquired.

I jumped, narrowly missing the large crack in the sidewalk on Wentworth Ave. "I didn't write it down, but I did happen to notice the title on his door just before I took my tumble. It read vice president of production. Why?"

"Why would the Vice President of production be the one to contract a dog catcher. I mean, doesn't it seem off to you that he would be the one taking care of such a menial task."

"I don't know; maybe they're not that big of a company."

"Are you serious?" Linda scoffed.

"What?" I shrugged.

"Happy Farms is third largest meat packer in the Midwest. They're the big David and Goliath story around here. When a larger corporation tried to buy them up, they refused to sell. The big companies banned together and started buying up more meat than they could even process, just so that Happy Farms couldn't get their hands on it," Linda explained.

"That's terrible. So how are they staying open?"

"I guess they figured it out," Linda looked at me puzzled. "I only saw the first story in the paper."

I patted Linda on the shoulder when we got to the park to let her know I was going to take a couple of the larger dogs out to the park and toss a ball around. I saw she was still deep in thought puzzling this out herself.

When I approached her again, breathless and tired this time, Linda's eyes were wide and eager. "What is it?"

"Do you think Tommy Bishop was in on it?" Linda asked.

I shook my head. "I can't see how. What possible reason would he have for wanting his friend dead?"

She offered a nervous smile, "I think we should call Deputy Hanson."

"What?" I gasped, not hiding my shock. "You? Of all people? You're not suggesting we tell him that Tommy did this are you? We have no evidence. We're just going to end up getting him in trouble and what if he did nothing wrong?"

"Okay, okay, fine!" she huffed. "Lordy, is this what I sound like every time you get cold feet?"

I snickered at her frustration. "Something's off about Tommy Bishop. If he's not our killer, he knows something." Linda said as her eyes met mine. "How would you feel about flirting with him to try and get some answers?"

"You just told me he was kissing Jill!" I snapped.

"Maybe they're not serious yet," she suggested.

"No, Linda! Let's go back to the coffeehouse, we're closed for the rest of the night, we can try and connect the dots there," I suggested.

"Can I have a blueberry muffin?" she asked and then laughed a little.

"You can have two, heck you can have six," I added, remembering the mountain of muffins waiting for us back at Half Day Coffeehouse. Linda nodded as she tightened her grip on the gathering of leashes. "I have so many dang muffins maybe all the dogs can have one too."

With that Piper took off at a full run, well as much of a run as a low to the ground Dachshund with abnormally short legs could. The leash pulled tight as she led the way for us.

CHAPTER EIGHTEEN

THE INTERACTION with Oliver Flank at Happy Farms shook me more than I cared to admit. I wasn't a detective. I never claimed I was, but even I could tell that Mr. Flank was unsettled by our presence. He clearly was hiding something. I had no idea if he was just caught up in the middle of something or if he was, in fact, much more dangerous. Worst of all, I had foolishly told him exactly who I was. I wanted to call Derrick, to tell him what Linda and I had been up to, what we had discovered, but if I did where did I begin?

"Do you think old Flank did the job himself or hired it out?" Linda asked.

"Huh?" I huffed, as I stared at the possible suspects we had written on a piece of paper. It formed an intricate web with all the arrows pointing back to Tommy Bishop and Oliver Flank. There had to be more to how they fit into the story, but a motive was escaping us.

"I think the man definitely had it in him to do the deed himself," Linda added.

I shook my head. "We don't know him. How can you say that?"

"Maybe not," Linda agreed, moving around to the fridge at the back of the coffee shop and removing a water bottle. "But I think we know enough to call in the Sheriff."

"Really?" I gasped, shocked by my ears. "Aren't you always the one telling me that the police in this town are too busy eating donuts to solve a case. That if you want it done right, you'd have to do it yourself."

Her eyes narrowed. "That's true, and I still stand by that statement," she paused. "But last I checked they were the ones that could actually arrest someone."

"Arrest someone," I blurted out. "Who on earth would we tell them to arrest? I mean come on, I saw a stray dog at a meat packing plant, and Jack's best friend knew the manager at Happy Farms. That isn't exactly what I would call damning evidence."

"Tommy," Linda muttered.

"We've been over this, I thought we decided that it wasn't Tommy that killed Jack." I snapped, growing impatient with the circles we were traveling in.

"N-no," Linda's voice quivered. "Tommy Bishop is looking in the window at us."

I swung around to look out the window, my breath catching in my throat seeing Tommy standing outside. He was waving at me and pointing at the door. I forced a smile and waved back. "What's he doing here?" I asked Linda, never letting the smile fall from my face.

"Maybe we were wrong," Linda whispered, despite there being no way Tommy could hear us on the other side of the glass. "Maybe Tommy did kill Jack, and he's here to kill us now."

He tapped on the glass impatiently before pointing at the door again and mouthing the words, "Let me in."

I turned my attention to Linda who now had her eyes

fixed on my cell phone a couple of feet from her reach. "What do I do?" I asked.

She looked at me through squinted eyes. "Should I call the Sheriff?"

Tommy was now standing at the front door, shifting his weight anxiously from foot to foot, looking around to see if anyone was watching him.

"No," I replied. "I don't think that's necessary." I quite possibly was making the biggest and last mistake of my life, but I moved around the counter and made my way to the door.

"What are you doing?" Linda hissed after me.

There was no time to answer her. The lock was already in my fingers, being turned. The door flung open, and Tommy raced in like a tornado.

"Lock it," he instructed, and I suddenly could feel my heart thudding in my chest. He raced from one window to the next, closing the blinds.

"Hey, Tommy," Linda called out as I moved back to my hiding spot behind the counter. "The Sheriff is on his way to pick up his nightly box of sweeties, he may think it's weird the blinds are closed."

"Sheriff?" he paused and looked over at me.

"Oh, yeah, the Sheriff," I added to her lie, though I feared not convincingly. "He comes by every night around the same time to get snacks for the station," I say as I look up at the clock on the wall. "I figure he'll be by in the next fifteen minutes."

The corners of Tommy's mouth turned up, and I couldn't tell if it was a smirk or he was just processing my statement. "That's plenty of time," he replied.

My imagination kicked into overdrive. Plenty of time for what? Plenty of time to murder Linda and me? Plenty of time to hide the bodies? Plenty of time to—

"Plenty of time to what?" Linda asked, glaring at him. Her mind was obviously fixed on the same haunting thoughts as my own.

He squatted, and I leaned over the counter to see what he was doing. I realized Piper had made her way to his feet and he was scratching her belly. *What was Piper doing?* I thought to myself, preparing to leap over the counter to protect her. He stood again. "She's a sweet dog."

"Thank you," I replied rubbing my head in confusion.

"You didn't answer my question," Linda reminded him. "Plenty of time for what?"

"To warn you?" he answered in the form of a question.

"Warn us or threaten us?" Linda shot back.

He shook his head in confusion. "What are you talking about?" He looked at me. "Didn't you tell her I already tried to warn you once?"

My eyes flew open in horror. "I—well, I—" My jaw dropped, words escaping me. He had told me I needed to stay out of the case and let the police do their work, but I wasn't sure myself if it had been a warning for my safety or in fact a threat.

His eyes traveled back to Linda, "I'm not sure what you think you know, but I was trying to help you two."

"Help us?" she scoffed. "The only thing that could help us is if you would quit being a coward and tell us something that would actually help figure out who killed your friend. That is unless there's a reason you wouldn't want us to figure that out."

"Linda!" I gasped, surprised by her sudden brazenness.

"Maybe I didn't want to say anything to you two because I thought you would make it worse, which is exactly what you did," Tommy growled, his head jerking wildly back and forth between us.

I glanced at my cell phone and debated if I would be able

to reach it without Tommy noticing me dial the Sheriff's office. Despite our story, the Sheriff wasn't coming, and Tommy's agitation was increasing—not surprising considering Linda's approach with him.

"Maybe we should all just take a deep breath and calm down," I suggested.

"Calm down?" he repeated my words. "I told you, but did you listen? No, you just had to keep pushing. I said if you knew what was good for you that you would stay out of this. Instead, you march straight into Happy Farms and tell them I spoke to you."

I hesitated. "No, we didn't. You never came up."

He squinted. "Wait, what? No, you had to of. How else could they have known we spoke."

I shook my head. "I don't know, but I promise, we never said your name."

Tommy huffed as he started to pace, lifting his hands to his head and running his fingers through his hair in frustration. "Oh God, what if they're following me? What if they know I'm in here right now?"

"Following you? Who would be following you, Tommy? Happy Farms?" Linda asked. "Oliver Flank?"

With that name his head snapped up, panic drawn across his face and confusion flickered in his eyes. "So you did talk to him?"

"Of course we did," Linda continued. "We're really are trying to solve Jack's murder."

"That's not helping," I warn her before shifting my gaze back to Tommy. "We did see him, but that doesn't mean you came up. Did Mr. Flank call you? Did he threaten you?"

"Threat is a word that's open to interpretation, apparently," Tommy scoffed.

I placed my hands on the counter and leaned forward. "Tommy, I wish you could see that all we want to do is figure out who's behind this. My life is on the line and based on your reaction I'm worried you think yours may be too."

His face softened as he lifted his chin and looked into my eyes. "I can't," He whispered.

My breath caught in my throat. He was close. He was about to break. I just had to push him a little more, I could feel it. "Did you know that Jack was working for Happy Farms?" I asked.

He watched me with guarded eyes. "Of course, I knew. I was the one that made the introduction with Oliver."

I could feel Linda silently taking in the interaction between us. Normally, I would have looked to her for guidance, but I had this. I sensed that Tommy trusted me for some reason, I only needed to figure out how to use that trust to figure out why he was so afraid.

"What was Jack doing for Happy Farms?" I questioned, unconvinced about the dog catcher story I had received from Oliver Flank.

He cleared his throat and began to fidget, shoving his thumbs into the tops of his pant pockets and then pulling them back out, "How would I know? Jack said he needed some work to bring in some extra cash, so I made an introduction to someone I knew that might be able to help him out."

Linda interjected, "Why did he need money? Was he in trouble?"

Tommy sighed. "The worst kind, he was in love with someone that wasn't in love with him. He had some crazy plan that he was going to buy the old Scarsdale place and fix it up, and once he could prove to his old girlfriend how well he could take care of her, she would want him back. It was all he cared about."

I remembered the engagement ring April had shown us. Jack hadn't taken her words as a final answer, he had instead heard and accepted a challenge. The Scarsdale place would be quite a challenge indeed. While the old mansion was owned by the city and could be purchased for a very modest price, the amount of investment it would have taken to restore it to an even inhabitable home would have equated to a small fortune. The complaints we had gathered about Jack stealing must have been him trying to raise the funds for his plan.

Pushing off the counter, I stood upright and crossed my arms. "Wasn't he at all concerned that his ex-girlfriend had a boyfriend now?"

Tommy laughed. "Brik?" He shook his head. "No, Tommy was certain April loved him, and once he could take care of her the way she needed to be, she would drop Brik in a heartbeat."

Perhaps we overlooked Brik too quickly. If Jack was that determined to win April back maybe Brik did have a motive for the murder.

Linda glared at him. "So, what's got you so spooked? If this Flank guy is your friend, then what are you so worried about?"

The corners of his mouth sank into a frown, and his eyes suddenly looked distant, staring off into nothingness. "I told Jack to cut it out. Oliver warned me that if he didn't, he wasn't sure what would happen to him," he rattled.

I bit my lip, and my body stiffened. "So, Oliver Flank did threaten Jack Egerton?"

"No—that's not what I said—not exactly," Tommy stammered.

"Then what exactly did he do?" Linda pressed as she turned to face Tommy. "And I'd hurry unless you want tell this story to the Sheriff when he gets here."

Tommy squirmed. After a moment of thought, he shook his head and inched back to the door as he spoke. "Look, I honestly don't know what they had Jack doing at Happy

Farms. What I do know is Oliver came to me and said Jack was trying to blackmail them. He told me I needed to relay a message to Jack that he had to quit, before he wasn't able to stop what was coming for him."

"As in he would have to do something to stop Jack?" I asked.

"No!" he exclaimed, then twisting his neck around in a circle, he released a frustrated groan. "I don't know, maybe. I didn't think Oliver could ever hurt anyone—but now I don't know."

"Did you tell Jack?" Linda inquired.

"Of course I did!" Tommy had become defensive. "But Jack wouldn't listen. He just said they were trying to get out of paying him, but he would make sure they paid up."

"What did he have on them?" I asked, my heart started to race.

Jack shook his head as he insisted, "I swear, I don't know. He wouldn't tell me." He stepped to the window and peeked out the blinds. Perhaps to see if he had been followed, or maybe it was to see if the Sheriff was coming thanks to Linda's phony story. "But then—tonight," He hesitated.

"What happened tonight?" Linda moved towards him as she asked the question.

"Oliver called me and said I shouldn't have been talking to you. I told him I didn't, but he said he talked to you and he knows that I told you everything," his voice cracked as panic consumed it. "He said that he couldn't protect you and that he wasn't even sure he could protect me anymore."

"Protect?" I grumbled, angry that I was being threatened by a man I didn't even know. "Who would Oliver protect me from?"

"I don't know, whoever at Happy Farms is trying to keep their secret. Please, Jack wouldn't listen to me, and it got him killed. Will you two just drop this?" Tommy pleaded.

I grimaced, watching as Linda curled her lip up for a moment. "We can't." Linda's voice had softened. "One way or another, Penny's life is over if we don't catch who did this. We have to figure out who killed Jack."

I frowned as I realized the hopelessness of the situation wasn't simply something I had been imagining.

He pushed off on his heels and dashed to the door, unlocking the deadbolt. "Fine. But don't say I didn't warn you." He began to open the door but hesitated for a moment. He turned back to look at me and with a sympathetic look said, "Good luck Penny Preston, you're gonna need it."

And with that, he was gone. Linda scurried over and locked the door after him, peeking out the window before returning to the counter and clutching her chest as if she were trying to manually slow down her heart rate.

"Now do you think we have enough to call the Sheriff?" Linda inquired, gasping for air after keeping her calm during the excitement.

I reached for my phone, "I'll call Derrick, he'll know what to do."

Linda smirked, then taunted me. "I'm sure Deputy Hanson will be delighted to help."

"This isn't the time," I stated as I continued to dial the phone and listen to the repeated rings. No answer.

∾

CHAPTER NINETEEN

I DIALED Derrick's phone number again and waited. I leaned against the counter, resting my elbows on the surface as the phone continued to ring. It went straight to voicemail again. This time I decided to leave a message. "Deputy Hanson. Hi, it's Penny Preston from the Half Day Coffeehouse," Linda smirked as I left the unneeded explanation of who I was on the recording. I waved a hand at her dismissively. "I really need to talk to you as soon as you have a chance. I'm at the coffee shop, now. Please call me back."

Linda rolled her eyes, and she shook her head.

"What?" I growled defensively.

"I don't know why the two of you don't lock yourselves into a closet for a good old fashioned make-out session already," Linda said, scrunching her nose.

"Don't start with that mess again," I warned her. I was a divorced woman for a reason. I am bad at relationships. When I say bad, I mean like atom bomb's go off in my wake, the end of my relationships are the end of the world as we know it—I'm that bad at relationships. All that is left when

I'm done with them is a wasteland. I couldn't do that to Deputy Hanson, it wasn't fair.

She grinned, pleased with the reaction she had gotten out of me.

"Maybe you should try calling the Sheriff," she suggested.

I tapped on my phone a couple of times as I considered her suggestion, then wiggled it into my back pocket. "I think we need to see him in person."

Linda's eyes widened. "I don't want to say you're nuts, but I'll ask—are you nuts?"

"It's hard enough to explain everything we've found out when we are looking at our crazy little diagram, I can't imagine trying to explain what we know over the phone. I say we just go. Besides, I have a hunch if someone is lurking in the shadows from Happy Farms ready to kill us, they won't want to head into the police station to do it."

"True," Linda nodded. "I'm game if you are."

I clapped my hands, and sighed. "It's decided. We're going to go to the police station, and we're going to tell the Sheriff and Deputy Hanson everything. I just hope it doesn't end with my arrest."

"As long as you go in expecting to be arrested, then it couldn't get any worse, right?"

"Always with the words of wisdom Linda, thank you," I pulled my lips tight into a fake smile as I stared at her. "Let me take Puddles out one more time and then we'll head out." Puddles was an eight-year-old Boston Terrier who had been raised by an elderly gentleman in town. When he recently relocated to a nursing home, there was no-one to care for his precious pup Puddles, appropriately named for the frequency with which she had to urinate.

"Gotcha, I'll just clean up in here quickly."

I walked to the door of the kennel, paused and turned to

Linda. "You know you don't have to go with me, I don't mind going to the station on my own."

"Are you kidding?" she exclaimed, scooping up several stray papers in her hands and placing them in a neat pile. "And miss all the excitement? No way."

I smiled, feeling relieved. "Thank you."

My mind started to run through what I would say once we got to the police station. Should I speak to the Sheriff, or would my news go over better with Derrick? I felt my phone begin to vibrate in my back pocket. With one hand, I reached for the door handle to the kennel area and with the other retrieved my phone. Derrick's name flashed across the screen of my phone as I stepped through the doorway, leaving the door to shut on its own behind me.

About time, I thought to myself.

"Put it down," my chest constricted, and I started to panic as I heard the man's voice. My eyes looked around until they fixated on Oliver Flank.

"Mr. Flank," I gulped, my finger hovering over the call button on my phone to return Derrick's call. He stood with his red scarf draped around his neck over his brown trench coat. It was him, I was sure of it now. There was no sinister mastermind at Happy Farms, threatening everyone. Oliver Flank was the one we had been looking for.

"I said, put it down," he instructed again firmly, shaking a small gun he held in his left hand at me. I immediately complied, placing it on the shelf above the dog cages. The dogs ... my mind when to them. They should have been barking their heads off with a stranger in the room, but they were silent. I looked around, each one lying down sleeping, not one aroused by Mr. Flank's presence. "You know, you really should have better locks and a security system installed. Anyone could break in here with the slightest of effort."

"Thanks for the heads up, I'll get right on that," I sneered.

"What have you done to them?" I asked, looking around at the cages again, inching toward poor Puddles cage.

"Oh, don't worry, they're no good to me dead, well ... at least, not yet."

"What are you talking about?" I asked again, debating if I could make it back through the shelter door and lock it before he could react. With his finger twitching over the trigger, I was certain I would be dead before I could touch the handle.

My thoughts were racing. Would Linda try to find me when I didn't reappear? If she did, I was certain Mr. Flank wouldn't hesitate to kill both of us. I closed my eyes, trying to connect with Piper. Usually when we interacted with each other, we were side by side. I wasn't even sure I would be able to through the wall, and if I could, it's not like Piper could communicate with Linda.

"You know, I wasn't sure if Tommy had told you anything. The way you got spooked and rushed out of my office I knew something had rattled you," Mr. Flank explained. "I called and told him you told me everything, that's all it took. He came scurrying right back here, didn't he?"

I shook my head. "No, you're wrong, Tommy told me he didn't know anything. He wanted us to quit investigating Jack's death."

He huffed. "Don't try to protect Tommy, he'll get what's coming to him eventually. I swear, you can't trust anyone these days."

"I thought you were friends," I grumbled, wishing I had placed the call to Derrick before setting my phone down so that he could hear what was transpiring.

Mr. Flank cleared his throat, rolling his head and cracking his neck. "Friends don't rat each other out."

My blood ran cold. There was no arguing with this man, he decided before he ever came here that the only way his secret would be safe is if we were eliminated. I had to stall for more time. Stall for an opportunity to run presented itself. "I promise, he didn't say anything to me."

"Can I ask you a question?" he asked, the way he looked at me was unsettling.

I shrugged.

"What was it while you were at my office?" he asked. "What was the thing that tipped you off?"

"What do you mean tipped me off?"

"Oh come on, don't pretend. I saw the way you raced out of there. Something rattled you. I'm just curious," he added with a half shrug.

The last thing I wanted to do was to be standing here having a chat with Oliver Flank. Well, actually the last thing I wanted to do was die, so I would continue to keep him talking. "The stray dog, it was the same breed that Jack and I had publicly had an argument about before he died."

He shook his head. "No, there was something else. It was after you saw the dog."

I thought about his question. "The picture of you and Tommy. When I realized how close you were with Jack's best friend, I knew it couldn't be a coincidence. But I promise, that's as far as we got. It's all circumstantial."

"Clever. You're right, none of it would hold up in court."

"Please, will you tell me what you did to them?" I asked again, looking around at the sleeping dogs, my heart growing heavy.

"Don't worry, they're just sleeping off a tranquilizer. It makes it easier to transport them."

"Transport them?" I sucked in a breath of air sharply, inching back and leaning against the door in case Linda tried to enter.

"If Jack had any sense he would have handled the job as efficiently as me," Oliver Flank sneered. "A sleeping dog doesn't cause problems. I mean, the entire reason you got a call about the stray that you and Jack got into a fight about, was because he wasn't doing his job properly.

"What job?"

He smirked, "Are you sure you want to know? I mean I have to kill you, but I'm not heartless. I would hate for this to be the last tale you hear before you got to the afterlife."

"Humor me," I replied, a slight eye roll followed my words.

He shrugged, waving his gun slightly, which caused me to flinch. "I hired Jack Egerton to catch and bring me dogs."

I nodded. "Yes, because of the problem at the plant, you told me about that earlier."

"You really are a gullible person, aren't you? Oh, sweet girl, he wasn't catching dogs at the plant, he was catching them all over town."

"But why?"

"So we could take them to our factory and feed them our hyper fattening food mix. In three weeks, let's just say those cute little pups you love so much will help us solve a meat crisis problem we're having at Happy Farms. Do you realize nearly four million dogs enter shelters a year? Over a million of those are euthanized. What a waste, I'm doing the world a favor."

My stomach sank, I was certain I was going to vomit. "What? You're going to kill them? You're going to let people eat—" I couldn't bring myself to finish the sentence.

"Of course we are," he spat. I had trouble seeing the kindness in him that Tommy apparently saw. "People don't care where they get their meat, as long as it's there when they are at the grocery store and at a price low enough to make them smile. Once I prove this pilot program of my idea is a success, it will become standard practice. Jack would have ruined all of that."

I shook my head, not disguising my horror. "You're not going to get away with this. People will figure out what you're doing, and Happy Farms will be shut down."

"And that my dear is why this isn't personal, but you're going to have to die. No hard feelings," he said as he cocked the gun. I closed my eyes, trying with everything in me to tell Piper goodbye and that I loved her. My thoughts were returned with the image of a clothes iron. An iron? Is Piper seriously telling me at this moment that I should wear less wrinkly clothes? I sighed. My life was young, but it appeared this was the end.

CHAPTER TWENTY

MY EYES WERE SQUEEZED CLOSED TIGHTLY, but there was no boom of the gun. I considered the possibility that he was having doubts. Perhaps I could reason with him. Too scared he was only waiting for me to open my eyes to shoot me, I kept them closed as I pleaded in silence.

"Please Oliver," I began, recalling a series on TV where cops used a perps name to gain familiar ground with them. Oh, wait. Maybe it was supposed to be my name I was supposed to say to make me a real person? I can't remember. "I am the only person in the world these dogs have. I'm begging you, if you just leave us alone I will never tell anyone."

"It's not good enough," he growled. "I'm sure you're very nice, but I don't have a choice."

I shook my head wildly, tears now streaming down my face. "No, you absolutely have a choice."

"If this ever got out I would be ruined. And they'd put me in prison for killing Jack." He laughed. "You know I only intended to scare him. He wouldn't listen. Then when I told him I wasn't going to pay his blackmail anymore, he said that he would just call the Sheriff and let him know what I'd been doing at Happy Farms. I warned him, but he wouldn't stop."

"So you stabbed him?" I asked through squinted eyes. I considered lunging for the gun, but my body felt like it was weighted down with concrete. A darkness threatened to creep in at the edges of my vision, but I managed to keep it at bay.

There was a mixture of disgust and fear in his eyes. He was conflicted, but only enough to slightly delay the inevitable. "Mr. Egerton made his own choice. He didn't have to be so greedy. I told him I was happy to pay him based on our original agreement, but it wasn't good enough. I told him we needed more dogs and fast if we were going to have any chance of meeting our first processing deadline. You must have really rubbed him the wrong way because after your little argument about that stray he suggested we clean out the dogs in your rescue."

"That's why he was here?"

His gaze was steady as he continued, "It was such a large haul of dogs I told him I would meet him here to help, but my true intention was to see if he could be convinced to see reason." He paused. "He couldn't."

"Reason? You're talking about killing dogs for food, how is that not insane?"

"Clearly you have trouble seeing the bigger picture Ms. Preston. I understand, most people will struggle with the idea at first, but eventually, people will come to see me as a visionary." He swallowed hard, lifting the gun a little higher and pointing it directly at my head. "I'm sorry it had to be like this."

I winced, just as I saw the door open behind him, throwing him off guard. He lifted his gun straight up in the air as he turned to see what was happening. There was a flash, and a boom as the gun fired. I caught a glimpse of a silver block flying, hitting Mr. Flank square in the temple. He stood stunned for a moment, staggering. The gun fell from his hand and to the ground, and a trickle of blood rolled down his cheek from a gash on his forehead.

As he fell, Linda was revealed, standing in the doorway with an iron in her hand and Piper standing at her feet, her familiar doggy snarl on her long-snouted face. "Did I kill him?" Linda shrieked.

Shaking off the shock I lunged forward, grabbing the gun and making sure it was far out of the reach of Mr. Flank before checking for a pulse. I shook my head, "He's alive. Get me those leashes," I instructed, pointing at the hooks behind her. "We need to tie him up just in case he wakes."

Five leashes later, we had secured his hands, legs, shoulders and ankles and the fifth leash was for his mouth. He was good at threatening us, and it grew old quickly—we took care of that by gagging him.

"Yeah, I don't think he's going anywhere," Linda commented.

I couldn't help but laugh as I stood and retrieved my phone to call the Sheriff. I saw three missed calls from Deputy Hanson on the screen of the phone. A little late, I thought with a grin. I swiped my finger across the screen of the phone, pressed Derricks name and listened for the ring. It sounded odd, though, as if there were an echo. I looked up toward the propped open rear door of the Kennel to see Deputy Hanson was standing there with his phone ringing in his hand, his mouth hanging open, and his eyes shifting from me to the body on the ground, and then to Linda.

"There you are!" I exclaimed as if I had been looking for him for days.

"About time," Linda coughed.

"What's going on here?" he asked, shoving his phone back into his pocket and entering through the door. His eyes moved from Flank back to me. I was on my knees with Piper planted protectively in my lap. "Are you okay?"

I smiled, relieved, and nodded. "Thanks to Linda."

"Don't worry Deputy, I won't make you say thank you for me doing your job and all," Linda teased.

I shook my head, my brow furrowing as I processed the situation for the first time. "Wait, Linda, how did you know he was in here with me?"

"Are you kidding?" Linda howled. "Your little angel there, Piper, was practically pulling me across the room to the door and whining. I pressed my ear against it and heard that old sausage fun factory man down there wanted to kill you, and that was it. I sprang into action."

I laughed at her choice of words. "You sure did."

"I headed upstairs and grabbed the first hard thing I could find, an iron." Suddenly the mental image Piper had sent me made much more sense.

"Kill you?" Deputy Hanson nearly shouted.

"Oh, yeah," Linda interjected. "I want to say that while I did hit him on the head with an iron, he did have a gun on our sweet little Penny here, so that was justified, right?"

"A gun, he—while I was—he," Derrick stammered, his face turning three shades of red in front of me.

"Deep breath, you can do it," Linda taunted him.

Puddles whimpered as she stirred in her cage, the effects of the tranquilizers starting to wear off. My head jerked back up to Derrick. "We need to call Dr. Abrams, he did something to them. They all need to get checked out." Dr. Abrams was the local vet, and he had a soft spot for the shelter. He often offered his services to us for free or at a deep discount.

Derrick swallowed hard, and sucked in a deep breath, exhaling it slowly. His composure regained he instructed, "Why don't you ladies go in the CoffeeHouse and call Dr.

Abrams while I show Mr. Flank to the squad car and call the Sheriff."

As the door closed, I saw Derrick pull Mr. Flank up onto his feet and mutter, "You're lucky you didn't harm those ladies, or this would be going down very differently." He then began to read him his rights, something I had never actually witnessed done in real life.

My face flushed hot, and I couldn't help but smile at the protectiveness Derrick displayed towards me.

∼

CHAPTER TWENTY-ONE

I THOUGHT the morning I found Jack Egerton's body was long, but the night Oliver Flank almost killed me rivaled it. After the Sheriff arrived, he and Deputy Hanson insisted Linda and I get checked out at the hospital, even though we were clearly fine. Then it was straight to the police station where countless questions awaited us.

It turns out the police were already aware of Jack's moonlighting job at Happy Farms, and had a hunch about Oliver Flank. The only problem was, they were having trouble figuring out a motive, same as us. I was happy to relay what Flank had revealed to me during our confrontation in the kennel.

When the police dug into the books of Happy Farms, they discovered that despite the story in the newspapers, Oliver Flank had somehow saved the company by resolving the plant's meat shortage. What he had been doing was purchasing retail meat from other companies and repackaging it. While it had saved the company from a story they may have never recovered from, it put the company in a financial situation that Flank knew would lead straight back to him and his panicked response to the situation, likely sending the company into bankruptcy.

In a desperate and delusional state, Flank came up with the idea to supplement their meat sources by fattening up stray dogs and turning them into ground meat. Much to everyone's relief, a room at the factory was discovered where Flank had been keeping the dogs until they were plump enough for maximum meat production.

Even though it had been a couple of weeks since all the commotion, business at the Diner had been staying steady. The story read like tabloid headlines, 'Coffeehouse Owner Foils Plot to Turn Man's Best Friend into Dinner.' After the morning rush, I took a moment to close my eyes, the scent of the freshly brewed coffee filling my nostrils. A calm settled over me, one I hadn't known since this mess began. I was finally starting to settle into my new normal. The door chime rang, and I had to force myself out of my relaxed state.

"Tommy," his name slipped from lips. I hadn't seen him since, well, since they caught Oliver Flank. I froze, waiting for him to make the first move. I didn't feel uncomfortable being alone with him in the coffeehouse just as I had known he wasn't the killer that first night when he was waiting for me at the back of the kennel. He looked well rested. His hair was combed, and he was wearing a tweed jacket that was slim cut and flattered his fit physique.

"Hello Ms. Preston," he smiled at me. He was fully composed and looked like the same old handsome bachelor I had seen come into the shop so many times before, though a little wearier around the eyes.

"I hope after everything we've been through you'll at least call me Penny," I answered, pouring him a coffee before he had a chance to order it.

"Fine," he nodded and offered a half smile. "Good morning, Penny."

I handed him the coffee and motioned to the cream and sugar. "Would you like a muffin or perhaps a croissant?" Okay, so calling what I made croissants was kind of a stretch. They were shaped the same and appeared to have a flakey consistency until you tore into mine and found the inside to be like a donut.

"Just coffee," he answered, his eyes fixed on me as he used the wooden stir stick. "You look good."

"Thanks, it helps when you're certain that a psycho killer is no longer on the loose, and isn't out there hunting you down," I replied.

He laughed. "Is that right?"

"Oh, yes. I highly recommend not being stalked."

"I'll keep that in mind." He searched my face as he continued. "Penny, I dropped in today because I wanted to see you in person and say thank you."

"Thank me?" I narrowed my brows as if confused. "I did nothing that requires thanking."

"I'm serious," he insisted. "You didn't have to take up Jack's case like you did. I know, I know, your butt was also on the line, but you saved more than just yourself that night."

I shrugged my shoulders and hissed, sucking air between my teeth. "You would have been fine."

He tilted his head. "You see, I—umm, well, I wasn't really just scared for us that night. I've been dating someone special, and Oliver had warned me that if something happened to him that she could get caught in the crossfire. If it wasn't for you, I'm not sure if I could have kept her safe."

I pretended I didn't know about Jill Egerton since he didn't use her name, "That is horrible, but congratulations to you finding someone special. I'm happy for you."

He nodded.

I lower my voice. "You know, I get that we're all glad

about catching Oliver Flank, but how are you handling all of this?"

"What? My best friend's murder, or my college buddy murdering my best friend? Don't answer that, I already know how messed up all of this is." Tommy leaned against one of the stools near the counter, not fully committing himself to a seated position. "I guess I've just come to terms with the fact that Jack was his own man and his actions are ultimately what led to his fate."

I smiled. "That's a very enlightened way to view it."

"Can I ask you a question?" he asked and I nodded my response. "How come you never suspected me?"

"Who says I didn't?" I smiled.

"Really?" he laughed.

I shook my head. "Nah, I'm just kidding. You just never struck me as a murderer. Besides if being weird was a reason to suspect someone, I would have suspected half the town."

"I'm weird, huh?"

"Isn't this entrapment?" I pleaded, lifting my hands into the air.

"I'm serious, if there's anything at all I can do to thank you, please just let me—"

"Actually," I drew out the word in a high-pitched tone. "With all the dogs we rescued from the Happy Farms factory we are having a puppy fair to try and match up these amazing and loving animals with their perfect forever home."

He raised a hand to silence me. "You captured Jack's killer, and I adopt a cuddly dog. That seems like more than a fair trade to me."

"Great!" I exclaimed, thrilled to see the seventh dog placed that day.

"You know the entire town is talking about how you and Linda just wouldn't stop until you brought justice to Jack. You two are the town heroes," he added.

"Oh, I don't know if I would go as far as saying heroes," I blushed.

"I would," Deputy Hanson's voice called from the entrance of the CoffeeHouse. I hadn't noticed the ding of the door, but now, looking at Deputy Hanson, I was at a loss for words.

"Derrick—hi, how ya doing?" Tommy bellowed patting Deputy Hanson on the back. Of course they were friends. Who in this town didn't know each other?

"You're not bothering Ms. Preston, are you?" Derrick laughed, eyeing his friend suspiciously.

"I was just about to ask her to marry me, but I guess I have to save that for another day," Tommy joked. He was not only handsome, but he had a sense of humor.

"I'm afraid her dance card is full right now," Deputy Hanson replied, glancing with a half-smile in my direction. My heart raced at his words. Was this it? Was he finally going to ask me out after years of mild flirting? "She's got a date with pouring me a cup of coffee." And suddenly my romance-filled thoughts died a quick death.

"Careful or you might just end up pouring your own coffee from now on," I glared at him.

"And that's my cue to leave. How much do I owe you, Penny?" Tommy inquired.

"On the house," I said with a nod. "Be sure to head into the kennel. Linda also has an area set up outside with some makeshift kennels in the parking lot. Once you find one, she should be able to help you out."

"What about law enforcement, do we get a discount?" Deputy Hanson asked in a flirtatious tone.

"No, I charge double," I huffed, sliding a mug across the counter to him.

I had been telling myself for years that getting involved with Deputy Hanson was a bad idea. I would eventually ruin things, and then living in a small town, we would likely run into each other frequently, and it would be awkward. However, since the night he arrested Oliver Flank, I couldn't help but notice how protective of me he'd become. I wasn't the type that needed protecting, but there was something comforting about knowing someone was looking out for me.

I moved around the counter with a wet towel to wipe down the tabletops. I felt Deputy Hanson's eyes follow me. He had me so twisted up in knots with his smoldering eyes and strong shoulders that when he brushed up against me accidentally, I dropped a mug from one of the cafe tables I was clearing off. It splintered off into a dozen pieces, scattering across the floor. I knelt with a huff to gather the broken shards, and Deputy Hanson quickly followed suite.

"Oh, you don't have to do—"

He didn't let me finish. "It was my fault, I bumped into you. I am so sorry. Please, let me pay for the mug."

"There's no need, I stole them all from the truck stop diner off 42."

He looked at me puzzled. "Huh?"

I shrugged. "Yeah, I go in every night for the midnight platter and put the extra mug on the table in my purse."

I watched as his mouth fell open. Emptying the ceramic bits into my apron, I shoved him in the shoulder and laughed. "I'm just messing with you."

He laughed, then began to fall back from my shove. He grabbed my arm to steady himself and the next thing I knew his lips were pressed up against mine. How you go from laughing to kissing, I'm not sure. It was all a blur to me.

We both lingered. It was one of those kisses that make you think maybe you don't ever have to breathe again. I mean, breathing isn't optional, but at that moment, you wish it was. When our lips pulled apart, we both just stayed, kneeling on the floor, staring at each other, speechless.

"It's about time," I heard Linda chuckle from the open door that led to the kennel.

The deputy and I stood up quickly. He turned red, made some excuse that he had to be somewhere, grabbed his coffee and fled as quickly as he could. I scurried to the trash can to empty the plaster chards into it.

"What was that?" she gasped.

"Nothing," I assured her, mostly because I had no clue what that was. "Aren't you supposed to be out back helping families find their newest cuddly family member?"

"Uh, yeah. Tommy is taking Puddles and Moe," she answered. Moe was the Mountain Dog from Jack's case.

"Excellent news!" I exclaimed.

"And don't you dare think for one moment that we won't be discussing that kiss later," she assured me. I ignored her, my face flushing red. "I guess I better get back out there."

"It feels weird, doesn't it?" I asked as she turned to walk away.

"What does?"

"Not being preoccupied with catching a killer."

"I know, I can't wait until our next mystery," Linda replied with a grin.

I laughed. "Yeah, right."

"I do think that we should see about getting our official private investigator license if we're going to make this a regular thing," Linda added, but was out the door before I could respond.

I looked down at Piper. "You hear that girl. She's lost her mind." An image fills my thoughts of myself dressed in a trench coat and Piper under my arm wearing a small dog sized deerstalker cap.

I busted out laughing in response. "Oh, no. Not you, too?" Despite my resistance to admitting it, I was warming up to the idea.

"Penny Preston, Private Investigator," I said out loud.

Linda popped her head from around the corner, where she had been hiding, "I'll get started on getting us registered for classes, right away."

"I—" The word hung in the air as I hesitated. Maybe it was the lingering effects of Deputy Hanson's surprise kiss or perhaps I was still on an adrenaline high from helping capture Jack Egerton's killer, but I replied, "We'll talk about it."

~

CONTINUE THE FUN...

O Deadly Night

Chapter One

"Do you have any more of those hard candy peppermint spoons?" I looked over my shoulder and watched Linda sneak another snickerdoodle thinking I wasn't looking.

The Christmas holiday season was here and the last two workers I hired were no-shows after only two days. I had begun to rely on Linda to help me around the coffee shop. She was cheap considering she wouldn't let me pay her an actual salary. Her only requirements were I keep the rent low on her apartment that was located above my coffee shop and where she ran her seamstress business. Additionally, that I would never withhold her access to free cookies and coffee. I accepted those requests asking only that she wait to partake in the free goodies until after there wasn't a line out the door on our busier days.

The women at the counter wearing holiday sweaters adorned with Christmas lights continued eyeing me up and down, whispering to one another. I assumed they had read the recent article written about Linda and I solving Jack Egerton's murder. I had thought the stir caused in our little town, and the attention to me specifically, had died down. Okay, poor choice of words. Nonetheless, by the summer the lookie-loos had faded away and life in small-town Wyoming, Ohio had practically returned to normal. That was true until Chaz Johnson showed up this fall with his flashy smile and spray tan asking questions.

Linda recognized him instantly as the Cincinnati journalist who was assigned the crime beat. She was also thrilled to answer all of his questions despite my reservations. It was nearly a month ago that the story had been released and honestly, I had almost forgotten all about it. That is until two weeks ago when the usual holiday rush brought people into town visiting our quaint little shopping district quadrupling foot traffic. Several customers had even brought in the article for Linda and me to sign.

"Linda," I hissed, trying to get her attention. Her eyes flashed wide as she realized she had been caught. "Do we have any peppermint spoons left?"

She sprayed crumbs as she tried to speak with her mouth full. Then accidentally sucked some of the crumbs down her airway, promptly launching her into a coughing fit.

"Are you okay?" I was partially concerned and the other part was annoyed.

She lifted a single finger in my direction indicating she needed a moment. I moved around her, checking the chiller myself to see if the latest batch of candy spoons had hardened. After confirming they were ready, I snagged two and returned to the register, placing one on each saucer in front of me.

"Whipped cream, ladies?" I had to raise my voice to be heard over Linda's coughing fit.

"And sprinkles," one of the ladies exclaimed excitedly.

"Just whipped cream for me," the other added in a more somber tone.

I feigned a smile, now quite concerned for Linda's well-being, as I fulfilled their requests.

"Can you settle something for us?" The quieter woman of the group leveled her stare at me.

"If I can." A creeping feeling slithered over my skin.

The excited woman with Rudolf's glowing red nose on her sweater leaned in and pointed at her friend. "She thinks the article was all a bunch of lies and that a lot of what was written was to sell papers. Is it true you found the dead body back there?" She looked at me while giving a few quick head jerks toward the door that led to the dog shelter.

I heaved in a large breath and forced another smile. "It's all true. And after you enjoy your mint mochas, I welcome you to walk back there and have a look at the exact spot where I found the body. While you're looking around, feel free to check out all the amazing dogs we have looking for forever homes this holiday season."

After Aunt Lily passed away, I was surprised to discover she had left me the building she owned on Main Street as well as the coffee shop on the lower level. I had already been working at the coffee shop, so that was a natural fit, but I had no experience as a landlord. When the unit on the first floor of the building went vacant, I decided to reinvest some of the funds Aunt Lily left me. I used the money to turn the space into something I had always dreamed about—a shelter for stray dogs.

The shelter isn't huge, and at any time I can only home a dozen dogs, but it's something. Something I can do to help unwanted dogs. There was an entrance at the rear of the building and I added another door to access the shelter and viewing window. It made it easier for the coffee shop customers to view available dogs. The constant foot traffic was a huge help finding homes for the animals. Although I hated talking about the murder I had witnessed there was one thing I couldn't deny; the publicity from the murder brought a lot more people to Half Day Coffee Shop and helped find many more dogs new homes.

"I told you," Rudolph sweater muttered under her breath.

"So she says." The other woman took her mint mocha and rolled her eyes, making her way to one of the few open tables.

I spun around, just as Linda finished taking a huge swig of water. "You okay?"

She nodded, trying to catch her breath.

"Snickerdoodles are a little dry today," she managed to say finally.

"Gee, thanks. It's funny that you ate a dozen before you noticed that." I counted the remaining cookies to confirm my suspicion and smirked at her.

Linda threw her hands up. "Hey, you know me. I gotta be honest."

"To a fault," I muttered just low enough for her not to hear me as I turned to help the next customer.

I no longer had to force a smile. Instead, the elation I felt peeled across my face exposing a goofy grin.

"Hi, Penny." Deputy Hanson flashed me his perfect pearly whites. At some point over the last nine months, we had graduated from calling each other by our surnames. Well, unless I was talking with Linda. I had given up with her. The poor Deputy would be referred to as Deputy Handsome until eternity.

"Hey, Derrick. What can I do ya for?" As soon as the words left my mouth, I wanted to erase them like yesterday's specials chalkboard, but it was too late. They were hanging in the air and there was no taking them back. I was a complete dork and if he didn't know it by now, he wasn't very observant.

Derrick cupped his hands and blew into them before rubbing them together. "Some gloves would be nice. Sheriff Wright put me on shopping district duty. I've been walking the strip. You never know when there could be a shoplifter."

I grinned at his obvious sarcasm. Wyoming wasn't the type of town people would try shoplifting. Of course, it was also never a place I thought a murder could happen, so what do I know.

"If it's any consolation, I feel safer knowing you're out there." I looked at Derrick from under my eyelashes.

"I bet you do." Linda snickered reminding me she was standing directly behind me. I lifted one leg to give her a swift kick in the shin. She yelped in response and then forced a smile at Derrick as he looked at her with a worried stare.

"What was that?" Derrick inquired.

"Huh, oh——" Linda had to do some fast talking to not blow her cover. "I said I bet you...I bet you haven't tried Penny's new peppermint mocha."

"Yes!" I gasped, ready to die from embarrassment. "I don't have any gloves to give you for your patrol, but this is guaranteed to warm you right up."

"Sounds good. I'll have one of those," Derrick replied as the door dinged again, signaling another customer. "You sure are busy lately."

"Yeah." Linda scoffed. "she hasn't been this busy since old Jackie boy went and got himself killed in the back room."

"Linda," I scolded.

"What?" She shrugged as she went to retrieve a peppermint candy spoon.

My beloved Dachshund, Piper, who I had shared a psychic

connection with since our near fatal car crash a few years back, popped an image of her licking a candy spoon into my thoughts.

I bent down low to where she rested in her bed under the counter and whispered, "Nice try, not happening."

Derrick shook his head. "She's fine. Speaking of, I saw the piece in the paper about you."

"You mean about the two of us." Linda corrected him as she wagged a finger between the two of us.

I blushed and shook my head. "I wish we'd never talked to that reporter." Meaning I wished Linda would have kept her mouth shut with regard to speaking to the reporter. "All this attention, they should just let Jack rest in peace."

"It seems to me the article was less about Jack and more about you. Oh, and Ms. Louise here." Derrick quickly corrected himself as he smiled at Linda.

"Whipped cream?" My brow arched and I couldn't help the slight frown that appeared on my face.

"Always."

I could feel his gaze pour over me. Linda placed the peppermint spoon on the saucer as I was topping the steaming cup of mint mocha with creamy whipped goodness.

"How much do I owe you?" Derrick asked. I would tell him it's on the house, but we had done that dance too many times. It always ended the same way, with him insisting on paying.

"That will be $4.25."

"Isn't it time for your break?" Linda suggested with a devilish grin.

"Huh?" I grunted as Derrick handed me exact change.

"A break? I would love if you joined me." Derrick looked hopeful as he reached for his coffee.

Linda gave me a less than gentle shove. I steadied myself and sighed.

"Uh, I don't know. We have a pretty long line." I couldn't help but grit my teeth at Linda.

"Bah!" Linda waved a hand at me dismissively. "I can handle this. Plus, you know how testy you get if you don't have your hourly injection of the good stuff."

"Coffee," I clarified what Linda meant.

Derrick laughed and came to my rescue. "I kind of assumed."

Before I could say another word, Linda was pouring me a mug of coffee with one cream and sugar, and pushing me toward the opening in the counter. She suggested we sit at the bar stools, whispering so only I could hear that it would be easiest for her to eavesdrop if we stayed close.

Linda wasted no time helping the next customer in line, and my stress about how busy we were disappeared for a moment.

"So." Derrick attempted to segue into conversation as we took our seats. "The article."

"Yes, the article." I lifted the coffee mug to my lips and took a tentative sip.

"I was wondering." He looked up and studied my face before he continued. "Do you think you'll have time to run the shelter, the coffee shop, be a landlord, and start your own agency?"

I shook my head in confusion before I remembered the part of the article he was referencing. Linda had told Chaz Johnson that we planned to open an investigative agency. The prospect was a gross exaggeration as it was something she had brought up a few times and I'd ignored all her efforts and suggestions.

"Oh, that." I laughed nervously.

Derrick tilted his head to one side and with a tender smile he added, "The town thinks you're quite the detective."

"My help in catching Jack's killer was a fluke," I insisted, shaking my head.

"I'm not talking about Jack's murder." Derrick shifted on his bar stool.

I saw Linda watching us over Derrick's shoulder as she poured the next customer a cup of coffee to accompany a slice of cinnamon bread. I was pleased that she was doing everything in the correct order. Despite her snippiness at times with the customers, Linda was the best non-employee or employee I'd ever had. If she ever gave up her job as a seamstress, I'd gladly offer her to work in the coffee shop full time.

"Then what are you talking about?" I asked even though I already knew the answer to his question.

After Linda and I played such a pivotal role in solving the murder of Jack Egerton, people started coming out of the woodwork asking for our help. First it was missing pets, then a woman who thought her husband was cheating. That one ended with good news because he was moonlighting at a second job so he could send his wife on her dream vacation for their anniversary. We even had one robbery case that wasn't a robbery but a case of one family member disagreeing with what they received in a relative's will. Consequently, they decided to take what they felt was rightfully theirs instead. Not exactly what we would call exciting mysteries, but we'd solved every case giving Linda the idea that we should start charging for our services.

My foolish response was that we aren't even licensed private investigators so it felt a little shady to charge for our services. Linda couldn't have agreed more, which is why she signed us up to take some classes to become licensed investigators. A juicy piece of information she was all too happy to share with our reporter friend, Chaz Johnson.

"It's a small town, Penny. I'm not sure how you thought

you could keep what you and Linda were up to a secret." Derrick spoke more directly, disapproval in his tone.

"Excuse me? What we were up to?" I snapped. I was a redhead and despite my shade being closer to auburn the stereotype of a short fuse rang true when it came to me.

"I'm just saying, it's not like you're fooling anyone." Derrick's eyes softened as soon as he spoke those words. I could see that he regretted saying them, but it was too late.

"I'm not trying to fool anyone. Maybe if you and Sheriff Wright worried a little more about the actual crimes here in Wyoming, people wouldn't come to us to solve them. Instead, you're out there looking for make-believe shoplifters. I think maybe it's you who isn't fooling anyone, Derrick Hanson." I could feel my blood start to boil. The detective agency was all Linda's idea, and while I didn't really have any intentions of following through on it, I did not need Derrick or anyone else weighing in on what I should do.

"Penny, I didn't mean to upset you. I'm just worried about you."

The flutter in my stomach told me I should be flattered and excited by his statement, but the heat emanating from my face told me I wanted to claw his eyes out for thinking I would even have the time or inclination to try and fool anyone.

"Excuse me," a soft but high-pitched voice rang out from behind me.

"What?" I bellowed as I spun around.

The Rudolph sweater woman was standing there with big doe eyes, and our newest resident of the shelter in her arms, a Pomeranian named Hank. "I-I'm sorry. I was... I just wanted—"

"I'm so sorry." I cut her off and stood, taking her arm. My expression softened as I looked at Hank in her arms. "I didn't mean to snap. Are you interested in adopting Hank?"

She nodded meekly as I turned and led her through the shelter doors, not saying another word to Derrick.

"I guess we'll talk about this later," he yelled after me before the door fell closed.

I had no intention of discussing the matter with him again.

≈

RECIPE

Easy-peasy Peanut Butter Cookies

A family favorite of ours...

One egg

One cup sugar

One cup Peanut Butter

Preheat oven to 350 degrees.

Mix all ingredients until smooth.

Roll dough into one inch balls and place on a parchment lined baking sheet.

Press a criss cross pattern on the top of the cookie using a fork as you flatten the ball of dough.

Bake for 10 minutes. Remove and let cool.

* Sometimes our family adds oats or chocolate chips to the cookies to mix things up. Always quick, easy and yummy.

ACKNOWLEDGMENTS

First I want to say thank you to my readers who encouraged me to go back and have an additional editor make a run through this book and release this revised edition. Your loyal support keeps me striving to always provide you with a better product. I wouldn't be able to do what I do without your desire to read my books. Thank you from the bottom of my heart.

A huge thank Amy Donnelly for always doing a great job editing my books.

To my mother, Linda Louise Allen, I dedicated the book to you, but that doesn't seem to begin to cover it. Cancer won't win because there is still far too much of an adventure in front of us. Fight hard and know you are deeply loved and we are all here to help you stand strong during this.

Thank you to my three kids, Zoe, Brayden, and Penelope who put up with a messy house and a lack of clean laundry so that mommy could write.

Lastly, Josh, thank you for pushing me when this book thing gets hard. I love you.

ABOUT THE AUTHOR

Wendy Allen, also known as Wendy Owens, was raised in the small college town of Oxford, Ohio. After attending Miami University, Wendy went on to a career in the visual arts. After several years of creating and selling her own artwork, she gave her first love, writing, a try.

Wendy now happily spends her days writing—her loving dachshund, Piper Von Snitzel, curled up at her feet along side their Boston Terrier Coco Chanel, and German Short-Haired Pointer/Lab mix, River Song. When she's not writing, she can be found spending time with her true love, her tech geek husband and their three amazing kids, exploring the city she loves to call home: Cincinnati, OH.

To follow everything current with Wendy Allen's Books:
www.wendyowensbooks.com
me@wendyowensbooks.com

ALSO BY WENDY ALLEN

Jack Be Nimble, Jack Be Dead

O Deadly Night

Roses Are Red, Violet is Dead

Made in the USA
Lexington, KY
08 March 2019